You just couldn't make it up!!

This is dedicated to all my fellow instructors doing a great job day in day out, taking abuse daily, you would think no one else had ever learnt to drive!

A huge thankyou to all the absolute darlings on our roads, as without you, this book would not have been impossible!

Let's also, throw in a bit of daily life, and of course, Social Media!

And, who would have thought, that in the middle of all this, that we would have The Coronavirus Global Pandemic!

Now that certainly is something that,

'you just couldn't have made up!'

Chapter One

Wow!

Life!

The daily strains, holding down jobs, looking after kids, partners, and a never-ending world of social media!!

How did we even manage before smart phones, social media, and the internet? It is all so much of our daily life's now.

Well, I shall tell you all how, shall I?

We actually got off our backsides, and went round to see someone, we didn't know what our neighbours had for their tea because 'rate your plate' didn't exist, and we either went to the library, or you ran upstairs for your encyclopedia if you wanted to find something out!!

We were also a lot more patience then, we didn't want everything now, right this minute!

That is exactly how...

Oh, and then we have Alexa...

Alexa, what time is it?

Just look at the clock..

And then, if you're really bored..

Alexa, what you doing?

I have been learning how to whistle and yodel, it's amazing what you humans can do with your voice box!!

Alexa, what you doing now?

I have been moving around the clouds singing to myself, tralalalala!! Ha ha!! As if!!

Who would even come up with an idea like that? Technology at its finest!

#Alexa!!

Do you ever think about when we were kids? How on earth did our parent's cope? They didn't have a clue where we were, or what we were doing, and not really any chance of getting in touch with us!

I for one would be worried sick if my son didn't have his phone on him! The worst thing is, when he texts me and says, "Mam, I'm alright, my phones dying, only on 1%" ffs Sam!! That's me not settling to you're in then! Bloody Kids!!

Personally, I love social media, and the internet, and if it used correctly then it is such a marvellous thing!

I know bad things happen, and to be fair, it is always going to happen, that' life, but it doesn't make it a bad thing.

I love to see what my old school friends and work colleagues are doing, and not because I'm nosey at all, just like to keep in the know and I'm interested in other people's life's!

And, I am one of those people that always 'like's' other people's posts, always comment, and generally just show an interest!!

Chapter Two

So, after spending an amazing 11 nights in the Dominican Republic, it's back to the grind….

Speaking of the Dominican Republic, I am pretty sure that if the kids had done half of what the adults had done in this 'Adults Only' complex, they would have been going mad!

But then again, it is 'do as I say, not as I do!' That's right, isn't it??

The absolute best one was clearing the long bar in the middle of the swim up pool bar, spreading ice on it, then the woman lying on the bar, whilst the men at either side grabbed an arm and a leg, then slid her forwards, then backwards, counting to 3, letting her go along with a big push, and then sliding off the other end of the bar into the water!!!

But at least 2 men were stood at the end of the bar waiting to catch the women, so they didn't smash into the edge of the pool!!

No health and Safety there my friends!!!

Anyway, all good fun!

No-one got hurt!

Definitely booking adults only to Jamaica next year!!!

Just landed at sunny Birmingham!!

Grab the cases, get the bus to the car park and let us get home!!

Why are you always in such a mad rush to get off the plane? but then, there's immigration to get through where you're queuing, and then it's a hour wait for your suitcases! We all do it though don't we? It's crazy!! Why??

After dropping to sleep for half an hour, I was thinking I was glad Jason's driving had been safe whilst I was sleeping bless him! It can't be easy having a wife as a driving instructor as I'm constantly looking around, checking traffic, watching him, and getting ready to brake or grab the wheel in an instant! Haha!!

He did once crash my car, and he was only at the top of the street, ffs! So, I think I have good reason!

The poor woman's car was a write off, and when Jase rang me, he said, "Kaz, I've just clipped a car at the top of the street!"

Clipped it? You've wrote the fucker off Jase!!

We are back in Castleford, barely awake, and I am conscious of the 2 suitcases of mucky washing and it is also a perfect windy, drying day! (It's quite sad that that's how I think about the weather these days, Oh, look at the weather, the washing will be dry in a couple of hours!!)

So, I check on my 24 years old son who has not long been in himself from watching Tottenham play Liverpool in the Champions League final. I don't think he enjoy the game as much as he would have liked when his friends support Liverpool, and he supports Manchester United!!

I am pretty sure that the second minute penalty put a right dampener on the stick he had planned on giving his mates!!

I had the usual, 'yes mother, glad your back and you had a nice time but, I'm tired, night I love you!'

Sam! it's 9am love, anyway, yes, night I love you!!

After napping for one hour, then scared to drop off again in case I didn't sleep at night, and, 3 wash loads later, (don't forget the good drying day) we had a KFC for Tea, 24 quid!! 24 quid for chicken and chips!! How do people even afford that? I could have had a right shop at Aldi for that if I hadn't had been so knackered!!

Little Alfie bobs, our gorgeous miniature schnauzer has been so out of routine whilst we have been away!

His routine is, sleeps in bed with us, wakes up at 5:15am and I'm like, "Alfie go back to sleep love, mummy is tired," I'm usually up at 5:45 to 6am with him, out for a walk to the end of the estate.

His shoulders hurt if he has long walks, so we don't walk him far anymore. As soon as we are back in, fresh cold water (he doesn't like it warm) a couple of chews and then it's a love whilst I'm watching the news, checking Today's Special Value on QVC (TSV), checking my online banking, emails and of course social media!!

It's funny how you can't remember life without a dog now! There is something I do know though, if someone would have said to me, that I would ever be sharing my bed with a dog, and, that I would have loved him like my own baby, I would have said that they had 'gone mad!'

But here I am, mummy to baby Alfie!!

Chapter Three

First lesson back and I feel refreshed and raring to go, chatting about my holiday and generally, all is good!

I am actually meeting myself coming back today if I am going to be honest!! Trying to get the washing out, rush to my lessons, and then shit! what about tea?

Thank God for the shop over the road! I will just grab some chicken, and I'm sure we've got a jar of curry sauce and some microwave rice in the cupboard that will do for today!

Remember Karen, you promised yourself you would be back at the Slimming club as soon as you got back.

Well, maybe I did but I didn't really anticipate how tired I would actually be, I will do it... one day... maybe... honestly, I will...

The consensus this week has been that if they've had a crap lesson, then it's my fault for being away for 2 lessons, but if they didn't, then they are really pleased because they can drive after a 2 week break!!

Either way, it's not really my fault anyway is it? I mean, let's face it, you're driving!

Tomorrow my son is 25 years old, how the hell did that happen!! Time just flies by...

It really isn't the same when you're not planning their birthdays months in advance, venue, party bags, cake, and inviting school friends, always trying to do something different, or something that their friends aren't doing, or have already done!

Thinking back, I think the best birthdays have been the bouncy castles in the back garden, buffet or barbecue, and of course, a bit of alcoholic hospitality for their parents! Like you do... don't you??

Not so sure why the adults always end up kicking the kids off the bouncy Castle, and then think they've all just become the best tag teams in wrestling!!!

I got him a card, and gave him some money and because I always struggle what to get him as a present, I still do like him to have something to open, so when I saw the 4 cans of Jack Daniels and Coke on then end aisle in the Asda for 4 quid, I thought 'perfect!'

This was, of course, when I bought him a Clive the Caterpillar Cake as all the football ones were a bit slanted, and at his age, I thought he might have realised that! After all, he's not 5!! Haha!!

On Monday, I asked Sam if he wanted to go out for his birthday on Wednesday, and he said, "well yes, but I was going out with my mates for a pint if that's OK?" "Yes, of course it is love, I was just asking, you go out and enjoy yourself..."

No! He wants to go out with his frigging mates, well actually Sam, 'no, it's not OK!'

The first time in 25 years we've not gone out for his birthday because he would rather have a pint with his mates!!

When did this happen? When did my one and only precious son decided he had outgrown birthday meals?

I'm not happy about this I can tell you!!

His mate pulls up outside to go out for a couple of pints, and I did feel a tinge not wanted anymore, but, then again, the apron strings have to be cut at some point don't they?

Alfie is having his monthly swim tonight.

He had been in pain with his shoulder, and the vets said that they could x-ray to see exactly what the problem was, yes and 400 quid later, no, thank you!

I decided to search the internet for any self help tips for my precious baby, and swimming popped up, hydrotherapy for dogs? Shut up! You can't be serious? A swimming pool for dogs? What happens here then....

The owner is actually a fully qualified physiotherapist on humans, and has transferred her skills to animals! Wow!!

His posture is so much better since he has been swimming, and he hasn't suffered any pain in the last 2 years, so that's all good!

Did you know that dogs can't actually swim?

We thought we would just take Alfie and he would just be swimming away, oh no, that's not the case at all....

After getting the vet to sign a consent form to say that Alfie has no medical issues that they should be aware of, I get to let my darling dog swim!

He put a little doggy life jacket on and splashed about wetting everyone through, whilst we both looked on admirably saying 'bless him!'

When a dog is 'doggy paddling' it is actually panicking, trying to find the ground, but moving along at the same time!

Alfie can now swim with his shoulders down, no splashing around, and in just a harness, not a life jacket! Go Alfie!

Friday, thank goodness it is Friday!

This week has been the longest ever! I've had a headache from hell, I'm sick of looking at a massive stack of ironing, it's chucking it down with rain, and I'm ready just have a couple of hours on my own doing absolutely nothing!!

Today marks 14 years since my lovely mum passed away, I was on holiday in Tunisia with my then husband Mick, Sam, and my nephew Brad.

I remember, we went back up to the room, and there was a note posted under the door asking me to ring home ASAP. I filled with dread, the kids were asking why? And myself, and Mick just looked at each other, whilst telling the kids not to worry…

The 6 weeks prior to going on holiday mum was in, and out of hospital, but was okay before we left for our holiday.

This happened in the day before mobiles were a common thing, and I went down to the reception to use the landline phone.

I phoned my sister Joanne, and said, "what's wrong?" She said, "Karen, I'm sorry, she's died..."

I remember screaming no! no! then some kind lady, who I had never even met before, took my hand and got me a brandy, whist Mick took the rest of the call. I cannot thank this lady enough, what an act of kindness from someone that you don't know, and, I have never seen her again.

I then went into 'Karen' mode. Right, I need to sort this, I need to get us all home, and be there for my sister.

The holiday Rep was amazing, she got us a flight home that night, we quickly packed, whilst wiping away the tears, and, then we got on the transfer bus, back to Monastir.

The flight seemed ages, and I could not wait to be home.

As soon as we drove into our estate and passed my mum's bungalow, I couldn't contain my tears any longer. My sister was so happy to see me, and the boys, and we just cried, while asking exactly what had happened??

Mum had been poorly all her life and blamed it on poor living after the war.

She had COPD and needed oxygen for 16 hours a day. Whilst she was asleep, she must have pulled the pipe out from her nose, and her oxygen levels had deteriorated.

Mum was outside her bungalow, and a carer that was going by, stopped, and called an ambulance. She got my sister as well, as we all lived on the same estate, again, an act of kindness from a stranger who I did not know.

There was nothing that could have been done for my Mum because her oxygen levels were too low.

Joanne was with her when she passed away, aged 64, its no age, it actually makes you realise just how precious life is...

Never take anything for granted.

Chapter Four

Absolutely tired as anything after a late night at the races for Jase's Birthday!

No alcohol for me, as I was the designated driver once again!

Since I have been doing this job, I don't really drink anymore, it's not really worth the risk, plus I work so many hours and I'm knackered!

I don't mind not drinking to be fair, I think we just live in a society now where its frowned upon if you don't drink, because everyone seems to be in the habit of nipping to the supermarket, or shop on their way home from work, and getting a bottle of wine, or 4 cans, or in my husband's case, a crate! Ffs!!

I reckon a drinking pandemic is looming, just like smoking related illnesses are now.. but, that is just my opinion!

Frigging bin men!!

I mean, I know that they have a job to do, but do they have training on been awkward? Or is it just me that gets so annoyed with bin men drivers?

Why can't they just move an extra foot forward so we can get by? It is so frustrating when they park away from the curb so you can't squeeze down the side, I'm sure they do it on purpose..

It's like, no love, he will have to take an extra 2 steps if I move a bit further down, then over the course of the day, he will have done 2 extra steps more than he should and we might have to call the union in to sort this out.. ffs!!

Quote of the Day from one of my lovely pupils..

Do you need a certificate to keep chickens?

Do you mean a licence?

No, I don't think so!

What do you think you do, get some chickens and then someone comes up to you and goes, ooh, well done, here's your certificate! Ha ha!!

Honestly, the things people say... or even how their mind works if it comes to that..

I did a mock test today, and there was a pigeon stood in the road near a parked car, my pupil is too busy moaning about the stupid pigeon, that he doesn't see a bus, yes, a big chuffing bus coming towards him, and by the time he realises this, we are blocking the road, the bus stopped to let him pass, he said, "ooh, that bus driver's kind letting me pass!" I said, "the driver had to stop to let you go through, because he couldn't get by because of the position of your car!" He said, "or yeh, good point! Shit, does that mean I've failed my mock test?" "Erm, yeh pretty much love yes …." Hahahaha!!

It always amazes me how people's minds work, and how totally different people can think the same shit!

We are approaching some traffic lights, and I said to my pupil, "at the traffic lights, straight ahead," so they said, "what, straight ahead straight ahead, or left straight ahead?"

So, I said "what??, What do you think I mean?"

"Erm, straight ahead straight ahead!"

Well Yeah! You know it love!

I mean where else would we be going, other than straight ahead? Well, who knows…but, she's not the first to say that!! Crazy!!

I will never, ever, understand why drivers act like dickheads around learners, but then again, its common on the roads driving now anyway, so you might as well get used it whilst you are learning...

An Audi driver comes racing up behind us, changes lanes, then cuts back in behind us, I said to my pupil watch this dick head! (like you do)

We went to turn right, and he shoots off straight ahead to the end of the road, he then turns right again, but we are already at the junction waiting to come out, so we pull out, and I looked in my rear view mirror and who's behind us? Yes, the dick head! Ha ha ha!

He had obviously tried to beat us, but was clearly unsuccessful, he then pulled up at the traffic lights, in the righthand lane, and we are in the lefthand lane, I just looked across at him, he looked at me, and I just nodded ha ha ha!

Go on lad!!

I suppose this job is quite important anyway, but we are also very trusted, and we are also affiliated to the DVSA who can revoke our Driving Instructor Licence at any time.

In my time doing this job, I have signed quite a few passport applications and never had a problem, so my son said, "Mam, how come you can sign passports, I thought it was just like doctors, nurses, and teachers, and that" I said, "well it is, it's anyone in a position of authority or, a recognised person" he said, "alright OK then". So, just to wind him up, I said, "well let's face it, I am a pillar of the community!" He said, "mum shut up!!" Haha!

But, even though I am joking with Sam, we actually are, and how many people over the years do you actually get through their driving tests?

Sometimes, it is a good thing that your pupils aren't aware of everything that is happening around them!

As we approached a junction, out of nowhere, came a druggie on a bike, no brakes, and he was struggling to stop! I'm just staring at him, my pupils too busy concentrating on the junction, she's totally oblivious!! thank goodness....

I know that she should be aware, but sometimes they will just panic, and slam on the brakes, and it is then us, that become the dangerous ones!

And this really gets me fuming...

Why, Oh, why, do some parents allow their kids to be so close to the end of the pavement? It is so frustrating!

A woman was watching her kid jumping into the puddles right on the edge of the pavement, and I was just watching the kid, she was looking at me because I am obviously watching him, and then they look at you, as if it's you that is in the wrong, for looking at them!! But, it only takes one little trip, and, that's it! Then who's fault would it be….

I am in a mad rush and today is no different!!

I call to put some petrol in in between lessons, I pull into the petrol station, and the guy in front is already paying, he can see me waiting, and then he just saunters out, has a look around before it gets in the car, then starts the engine, then put his seat belt on, looks at his passenger, ffs, just move will ya mate, I haven't got all day!!

Why the fuck do people do that!! It is so annoying!!

Then, the cashier is pratting about, just stood in between 2 tills, I said, "is it this one?" She said, "yes love it is" then I said, "can I have a receipt?" She said, "ooh, hang on a minute love, here you are" "cheers love, thanks see ya"….

Bloody hell, just be quick!! I haven't got all day!! I am, actually working, and should be at my next lesson now!!

Today I thought I'd have a nice chill out afternoon, so I had my hair done, nails filled in from my holidays, and then try, and promote Jason's flight simulator business!

I thought I will get a Father's Day balloon, and tie it onto the mobile advertising board outside the simulator, then when people pass by, they might call in buy a voucher!

I was thinking if one of them kids nick it when they get off the school bus that will be it!

Anyway, I called up at 4:30pm and it is still there. I am talking to Jase in the simulator office, and this guy walks by, he must have been in his thirties, looks at the balloon, walked past it, and then comes back again, rips the balloon off the bar and walks off with it!

I am absolutely fuming!

I ran outside and shouted, "hey up, what do you think you're doing with that balloon?" He said, "I thought it was just caught up on that thing" I said, "well it isn't, give it back it's not yours!"

He just stared straight at me and said, "come and get it" so, I walked towards him, and he let the balloon go... obviously, it's just floating away into the sky, and I said, "you absolute prick, why would you do something like that?"

A guy pulls up in a van opposite looking to see what had happened, and I said, "he's a thief! He's just nicked my balloon!" And all the time, it's just floating away, into the Sky, but, to be fair, I would rather nobody have it than him who tried to nick it!

And, all this time, my husband is sat inside the building, letting me deal with the thief!!

Cheers for the support husband!! Haha!

What actually is it with car park one-way systems??

They are there for a reason, for safety and clarity, but clearly, they should only be used when there is an empty carpark... erm, No!

I thought I would just nip to our local shop, and it's a one-way system, so all the cars are parking the same way, I saw this space that I wanted to go into, and, I'm just about to pull into it, when a car comes flying in from the wrong direction, and pulls into the space!

I just shook my head at him, and gave him a massive dirty look!

I then went to park in another space, and someone had parked too far over the lines, so I couldn't get in that, I'm like FFS!! Do they want a lesson??

When I went into the shop, I could see the guy looking at me who had parked in the space, and I'm like, Karen love, just leave it, it's a parking space, get over it! But I couldn't!! I was stood there in the queue, just staring at the back of his head, thinking Dickhead! Absolute, Dickhead!!

But how bad is it when they do that, and then, thinking there right smug, it is so annoying!!

This morning I thought I would nip to the 8am slimming club group, I'll just 'nip in' get weighed and out, surely it won't be that busy??

Jeez…. Old women pratting about in queue!!

Ffs! I actually thought all these just went to an evening class, why the fuck would they prat about on a Saturday?? And, then when I go to get weighed, I've lost half a bastard pound after all that!!

Fathers Day.

Days like these can be so hard!

My dad was only 48 years old when he died, and I was 23, he has missed out on so much in our life's, he never saw my son, and it hurts like hell, but, unfortunately that's life, and no matter what life throws at you, you just have to crack on, as hard as it is, there is absolutely nothing you can do about it!!

Chapter Five

Well, there has been this, well known, branded hairdryer, on the shopping channel for months now, but its £300!!

300 quid for a hairdryer!!

Now, can I actually justify that???

Who the frigging hell pays 300 quid for a hairdryer?? I am really tempted to say the least!!

I mean, all the presenters have them, but 300 quid…. I have read all the reviews, and to be fair ,they are mostly 5* but, it is still a lot of money for a hairdryer!!

Anyway, forget about the stupid hairdryer you cannot seriously even contemplate that, just get that city break to Venice booked for your 50th Birthday Year!!

Oh dear, after putting a post on social media about the justification of the hairdryer, it seems my friends have them, and, they are amazing! Ffs! that's it now, I will definitely want one!

I am so tempted, and its 6 Easy Pays of 50 quid… mmm….

And, a 30 day money back guarantee, if its shit, save the original packaging and all that!

Anyway, if no-one cancels next week, I might get one, but it is still 300 quid…. And… can it actually be that good? I mean come on, that is a lot of money!

What is with this weather it has been absolutely, atrocious since I came back of holiday!

My car needs hoovering out, but it has been chucking it down for weeks now, and I know it might be a bit of an excuse, but what a shit of a job hoovering the car out is!

I absolutely hate it with a passion, one of the worst jobs ever!

It's the same with it actually been washed, part of me thinks, what is the point? It is only going to get mucky again anyway, but, that's not very professional is it? But, then again, neither is just cleaning the number plate Karen love!

Well, its bedtime… still contemplating this bastard hairdryer! I'll sleep on it….

Why do people just see a red light, and automatically slam on!! Ffs!! And, this is not, one of my pupils, it is a full licence holder, I was fuming!

They were turning right, and just looked up at the light, which was for the traffic to their left, and bang, slammed on, I pipped my horn, and they were just pointing to the red light, and I'm pointing to all the traffic behind, they did eventually move, but honestly, it is ridiculous, people just need to think about where they are, and if the red light is actually for them!!

Cancellations are an absolute nightmare in the Driving Instructing Industry.

It is just not fair, and people don't seem to realise that this is how you earn your money, this is your wage.

Today someone cancelled because SKY has gone out of her account and she's overdrawn so she can't have her lesson, ffs, what do you do?

I mean, the only solution is to charge no matter what, regardless of the reason! But then again, if they haven't got any money, they haven't got it!

Its 26 years since my dad passed away at only 48 years old, I was 23, my whole world was turned upside down, how on earth do you get through that?

Life can be so cruel, but you just can't change it.

I have never experienced pain, and hurt like that in my entire life, it is truly heartbreaking, someone who has been there for you totally in your life, protected you 100% all the time, and then bang! Gone! Just like that!

No time to say goodbye, no time to tell them how much you love them and how proud you are to be their daughter, how grateful you are that they had given you THE best childhood ever, and now they are gone forever...

My dad never saw my son, and that's heartbreaking too, he missed out on all the good things in all our life's, it is so hard.
I know he would be so proud of all 3 of his grandsons, and he would have loved been a fantastic grandad to them, watching them play rugby, football, and cricket, he would have been their biggest fan!
When me and my sister played rugby league 30 years ago, he never missed a game he was always on the side lines, cheering us on, and, extremely proud!
He was so proud of us, and supported us unconditionally, just like I am proud to be his daughter.

Yyaaayyyy! We have a test pass today!
It was her second attempt, and to be fair she should have passed on her first attempt, but the examiner jumped on the brakes at a notoriously bad junction, and

she was minutes away from the test centre, and, that is all she failed for!

It can be so frustrating at times, a little chat about mirrors from the examiner in the debrief, and I really do like it when an examiner still takes the time to talk about their test, even though they have passed.

Where the actual hell is all this rain coming from? We are in June for God's sake!

I really do feel for all these poor people that have had their homes flooded, it must be, absolutely heart-breaking.

Oi Oi!! I have ordered the Hairdryer, fuck it!! 300 whole chuffing quid!! 300 quid!! Must want my head seeing to!! You only live once don't you!!!

I haven't found the right time to tell the husband yet, this needs to be done at the absolute right time, to ease any unnecessary conflict! Ha ha!

It is okay though, it is on easy pay of 50 quid a month so that makes it okay, right girlfriends??

Anyway, if its crap its off back, no messing!

If I'm going to be quite honest, I can't wait for it to be delivered, and actually use it!

I mean, for 300 quid, it is going to be the best right?

300 chuffing quid, oh my....

Had a quote today for our guttering, fascia's, and windows cleaning, basically all our upvc, I've asked my neighbours if they want theirs doing too as they are quite elderly, so now, I get the quotes, as they just can't be bothered anymore!

To be fair, I am still trying to redeem myself from when we had our fences done! Our fence was quite old, and it blew down in the strong winds.

I saw this small local business, and decided I would ask them, we decided on a straight edge fence and my neighbours had a curved top, they were not happy with their fence at all, but ours was perfect!

My neighbours said they would have to "titivate" it, titivate?? What a word... *titivate* haha!!

I so hope this bloke does this job well, otherwise my days of getting quotes will be numbered..

Hi Karen,
You've been recommended by a friend for driving lessons, do you have any availability please?
I'm available Monday to Friday after 5.30pm, Saturdays and Sundays.

Regards Jane x

Hi Jane,
Thanks for getting in touch, I'm really sorry I don't have any availability, as I don't work after 5pm, and I only do a couple on a Saturday, sorry!
Regards Karen.

Hi Karen,
Thanks for the reply, you don't work after 5.30, or weekends? Wow are you part time! Xx

Hi Jane,
No, I'm not part time, I work 7.30am to 4.30pm Monday to Thursday, and I don't work Friday afternoons as the roads are a nightmare, and my Saturdays are full, I do need some time off! Thankyou Karen x

Hi Karen,
Yeh, sorry about that just thought you would work evenings and weekend to accommodate workers!
Thanks Jane xx

Hi Jane, no sorry I don't, have you tried James Wood? He works evenings and weekends.
Thanks Karen x

Hi Karen,
Thanks, I will try him xx

Ffs!! Do we not need any time off?? We are only human, I could honestly work 7 days a week, 12 hours its crazy!
And yes, the money would be great, but, I would probably be dead!!

I mean evenings and weekends?? Don't you think we are stressed enough, without doing the extra shite of rush hour traffic and weekends!!

My first lesson today, wanted dropping off at college, instead of at home, so because I wouldn't have time to go home for some breakfast, I called to the fast food place.
Actually, how long does it take to make some porridge? Well, I will tell you!!
10 minutes, yes! 10 bleeding minutes for some porridge!!
Honestly, I had to eat it on the way to my next lesson, and its always 600 degrees boiling anyway, and, all I can say is, thank goodness for the tractor in front so I could eat my porridge!

We have a new road in our area that has a speed limit of 30mph but to be fair it should be more, but it isn't, and of course we have to abide by this!

I just got near to the end of the road and a car overtook me, but there was another car coming towards them, so she braked, but then I had to brake more, to avoid this silly cow been in a head-on-crash!!

I just looked at the driver that was on the other side of the road, and she was just gobsmacked! When we got to the traffic lights, she transferred back into the left-hand lane, which was the lane I needed to be in, but, I was that mad, I went into the right hand lane, slowed right down at the side of them, and we both had our windows opened a bit, and I said, "what the chuffing hell did you think you was doing then, how stupid, absolutely disgusting driving!!"

Then, just to top it all, when she drove off, I noticed she had kids in the back!! Wow!! Just Wow!
What an absolute idiot!! Why would you do that to your kids to gain absolutely nothing at the end of the road!! People just cannot wait!!
Why risk your life and others? It never ceases to amaze me!!
What a day!!

Why do people just think that it is acceptable to park where they want!!

We were waiting to turn right at a junction onto a busy main road, and a big concrete truck had parked on the wide pavement, yes, the pavement! And we could not see a thing, what an idiot!!

My pupil was panicking because we had to edge further and further, out into the road, but the cars were still coming down, and then, someone wanted to turn right into our road, so we had to be careful to not go too far out!

We eventually got out, and my pupil was then panicking if something like that happened on his test!! Some people just have no consideration for anyone else at all…

I had someone on a lesson today, and it was her son's sports day, so we were just chatting, and I asked her, "if he would win, or if it was non-competitive?" she said, "its non-competitive and they can't even run they must walk!"

What is wrong with people? No wonder we are raising a generation that gets offended so easily!! Life's not fair, and we need to get used it!!

If you lose, you lose, get used to it, and get over it!!

Quote of the Day!

"I'll pay you for 2 lessons, I'll pay you 27 and 27" "yes okay love",
"right then, can we call to the bank? I'll pay you 2, 27's"
"yes okay, so £54?"
"Is that what 2, 27's are?"
"Yes love"

"so 2 x 27 is 54, or is it? I thought it was 34!"
"No, its 54!!" Tell me what you do for a job again?
"I don't do maths though!"
"I didn't ask you if you did maths, I asked you, what you for a job"
"or okay... well I work in a nursery and not a school, so my kids don't do sums that big!"
Ffs!!! Haha!!

So, again, what actually is it with people with kids and babies on the road???

First thing this morning on a lesson, we had just come over the brow of a hill, yes, the brow of a hill, and we had to slam on because a man was walking on the road pushing a baby in a pram, and the woman was walking on the pavement!! Ffs!! What actually do people think these days?? What actually goes through their tiny little minds?

It is actually beyond belief!!

Anyway, we overtook them, slowly, and I had my window down a bit, so I said to him, "really, why not use the pavement?" They both just looked at me like I'd fallen from Mars! Clearly, I was in the wrong for been on the ROAD in a CAR, whilst they pushed their baby in a pushchair, on the road, when they could have all walked on the pavement! Unbelievable!!

Another idiot…

I am waiting to cross at a busy pedestrian crossing in our town centre (as a pedestrian) and these 2 women stopped at the side of me. One of them, then pushed the pram out into the road slightly, so, I look to her side, like wtf!! Then, as if a bus comes round the corner really close to the pavement, she pulls the pushchair back, but then goes to cross in front of a car, that's just come round the same corner!! I just looked at them both and said, "as if!!" She pulled the pushchair back for a second time, and then just ran across in front of a car with the pushchair!!

I just shook my head and said, "what an absolute idiot!" The woman at the side of me said, "bloody stupid!!"

We then proceeded to cross, when the green man came on..

Now my son is 25, and if we go anywhere I'll say, "you walk here love to this side" he's like, "ffs mam shut up, I'm an adult!" And I'll say to him, "I don't care you're still my baby, and I'd rather a car hit me than you, so shut up!"

Isn't that normal?

Isn't that what any parent would do?

Am I still overprotective?

It is all about 'ifs', 'what if??'

Anyway, never mind about work, and idiots, guess what got delivered today? Woop Woop! Yes, the 300 quid hairdryer!! Come On!!

I Still can't really justify it like, but 6 easy pays of 50 quid, and let's face it, it is only like what my hubby spends on beer and cigs in a week… that's my justification!

So, just in case, I have kept all the original packaging because if its crap, its off back!! 3 hundred chuffing quid…. I'm not exactly going to chuck that in the back of the cupboard.

Decided today that I really do need to paint the fence, it doesn't look like anyone else is going to do it, does it??

I started on the back fence, and on the panel that looks on to the field behind us, so off I trot up the street with my paint and paintbrush, and onto the field.

The sun was absolutely sweltering! I did 2 panels and honestly, I had well had enough!!

Got up at 6:30am with my darling little Alfie bobs, had a coffee, then 7:15am I am back out on the field painting the fence!

My husband text me at 8:30am to say he was setting off for work, FUMING is not the word, you haven't even been to see me, ask me if I'm OK? do I need a coffee? is it going on okay? what a prick!

Sometimes, I just feel like it's me that does everything, and he just goes to work, his day off is a total day off, on the game machine, or just sitting on his backside all day! Mine is cleaning, washing, ironing, general dog's body, and now to add to my never ending talents, fence painter!! Ffs!!

So, this is the second time I have used my 300 quid hair dryer! Haha!

I decided I would use my usual product on my hair, I kind of styled it, but then left it a bit, and then, just straightened my fringe a little, my hair looked amazing, and my neighbour even commented that my hair longer and blonder!

I think she nearly had a heart attack when I told her I had a new air dryer that cost £300 and that's why it looks amazing she said, "wow! and so it should for that price" Bless her!!

Why would someone on a scooter have music blasting out?? Ffs!! Can he even hear it? What a Dickhead! Haha!

Chapter Six

Since it was brought in that we could take learner drivers on the motorway, I will admit, I have taken quite a few on!

We have a good motorway network locally including a smart motorway, so, it's all good practice.

The ruling is that it must be with a *fully qualified instructor in a dual control car* I mean, is this a good thing, or a bad thing?

Personally, any extra difficult road driving is always extremely good for them, and, makes them more experienced, so when the person gets on all different types of roads, it can only be beneficial.

People would always say, "When I pass Karen love, I will have some motorway lessons, make sure I have some motorway lessons" but many of them never do!

But, today my pupil has loved it!! She wasn't very confident, and sometimes it can just be the boost they need, and after that, her confidence was sky high, and she was buzzing!!

We have an outlet village in our town and the roads that lead in and out are on test route so we use them roads quite often, but you can guarantee that people are never in the correct lane!!

Today a car cut straight across in front of us, 2 lanes in total, and we had to brake quite harshly, so when we stopped at the traffic lights at the side of him I looked straight at him, and clapped my hands, and said, 'well done!!!' He just looked at me, I bet he was really thinking, look at you, Mrs driving instructor there, thinking that she's queen of the road!! Haha!!

But, it is so frustrating, but, then again, it happens all the time, so my pupils have to be ready for every eventuality!!

It was very interesting to hear this week, that we cannot have barbecues anymore, as it is damaging the environment!!

Burgers take a lot longer to cook than a vegan style burger, so it's okay to cook them!

The presenter on one of our local radio stations was talking about it this morning and he said, "I think I'm going to lock myself in a room and just eat ice!" so I tweeted him (like you do) haha! And, I said that, "he can't do that because we need to save water!!" He then tweeted back with, "damn I forgot about that can I eat mud?" I tweeted back "yes, that's okay!"

An ambulance passed us whilst on a lesson and then about 5 minutes later we passed the ambulance tending to a woman about 100 yards down the road. About 6 kids and a dog came around the corner, and I said to my pupil, "hey up, I bet their mother has sent them out to find out why the ambulances is there!" haha!

I can remember my mum saying that to us, "quick kids, go up and see what the ambulance is doing!!" mothers will never change!

Near the test centre, we have a stop junction, and it has traffic lights just after it, to the right. When you pull out, if you are turning right, there is just enough room for one car.

We pulled out of the junction and a van came flying up behind us, but, because of the position of his van, and the constant revving of the engine, I said to my pupil, "just watch what's this dick head is going to do!" Sure enough, when the lights changed to green, he shot up from behind us, and overtook us, whilst we was just setting off and sped off!! We then followed him, and he stopped at the sandwich shop, which is about 200 yards up the road, now if he was going further, I could have understood it, but bloody hell, just to go to the Sarnie shop!!

Anyway, I looked at him, put my thumbs up pouted my lips and said well done!! He just looked at me like I'd lost the plot!!

So, we are going down a national speed limit country road, and there is a man jogging coming towards us, which is fair enough, he's facing oncoming traffic, but then we need to slow down because there is a car coming towards us.

The jogger kept on running towards us, but, by this time, we have literally had to stop, due to the other car, and there not been enough space to overtake him safely, and, not be a danger to the oncoming car, but, the jogger is looking at us and pointing his finger as much to say, what are you doing??

We have to swerve around him, to avoid him, when it's him, that is carrying on moving, and nearly causing an accident!! Honestly!! Some people are just crazy!!

Still on the same lesson, a big forty foot waggon pulls out in front of us at a junction, and proper speeds off in a 30 mile per hour road, he whizzes around the roundabout, and the cars have to just stop!!

Then we are in the right-hand lane, and it's not very often that wagons use the left lane to go down the narrow road, so again, I said to my pupil "watch him! He's going to come into this lane!" and nothing as sure, what does he do?? Pulls in front of the vehicles, and gets his foot down!!

Honestly, he must have been late for his drop because he was driving like a right idiot!!

Well for the first time in my 49 years I have had my false nails soaked off I was a bit scared at first and didn't know what to expect!! Anyway, I survived, and now have a nice fresh set of baby pink acrylics on!!

It's mad how you worry about little things like that isn't it? I mean, what if my actual nails would have dropped off!! Ffs!!

I really cannot get used to the shopping chanels today special value being at 9pm now, and not 12am!!

What do I have to look forward to when I get up in the morning? I am in a bit of a routine!! Haha!!

Well, we just came around the corner and found a van parked up, and 2 men were cutting tree branches in the middle of the road!!

We slammed on, and had to swerve around them!! I was just shaking my head!!

What actually does go through people's minds?

It was so dangerous, they just don't think!!

Today is not a good day, cancellation, after cancellation, after cancellation! I know it might only be 1 lesson to them, but when 6 people cancel in a week it is a lot of money lost.

Learning to drive is a commitment! The most frustrating thing for me, is that I only do set days and times for students, so that they know where they are, they can plan things around their lessons, and, it also fits in well with their lives!

It is always difficult in the school Holidays anyway, even people out of College, who have jobs, and, they just say to their employer, 'yes I'm available whenever!!' Well, actually you're not love, are you, because you've got your driving lesson!!

Or, mums just think, you know what, I can spend my driving lesson money on taking the kids out, but what about my kid? I need some money for my kid too!

And then you get all these that just don't give a shit, and just cancel anyway, they just don't realise it's your job, it's how you earn your money, and the most frustrating thing is that if someone cancels mid-morning, and you can't swap them for anyone else, you just have to go home, and sit at home for one hour, and then, go back to work!! That absolutely does my head in big time!!

I do have a cancellation charge, but, it's only 24 hours, if people cancel before then, then what can I do? Not a lot, except make sure that the ones that mess you about, are the first out of the door when you have had enough, and you get another pupil to fill that slot!

Oh Yes!! There are ways and means!!

I had a driving test today, and he was so nervous bless him! I tried talking to him about his driving, and how good his driving was, and, that he could do this!! Especially after previously failing because he went to move off when a vehicle was coming, and the examiner stopped him and said, "mate, you can't go there's a car!" and he replied, "yes, I know!" so the examiner said, "well why did you set off then??" ffs!!

But, anyway, I said to him, "what's matter with you? why are you nervous?" he said, "no, I'm not nervous, it's just my nerves!" "yeah, I know! Same thing that mate!!" Haha!!

3 lessons today, then I am done!! Sod it!!

This week can just go do one!!

I have had enough!!

We come to a stop at a pedestrian crossing, and, there is a little westie dog on the footwell of a mobility scooter, and, me and my pupil both said "or bless, look at him sat there nicely waiting for his owner to come out of the shop" but then, we noticed he had only gone and had a big shit on the scooter in the footwell!! Ffs!! Haha!!

We just started laughing and then we were laughing even more, when I said, "well, let's just hope the owner sees it before he steps onto the scooter" Absolute Classic!!

So, driving about you see all sorts, and you also get used to seeing some people about too. Now, the first part of this is quite serious, because, there is a young woman in my hometown who clearly, has drug and mental health issues.

I've seen her in some right states, and once, I had to stop in the middle of the road, because she was having an argument with her boyfriend, they were both absolutely off their heads, arguing, and fighting in the middle of the road, it was crazy!!

She also wears some really, silly outfits, and sometimes she wears wigs, including a bright orange one!!

But, anyway, she has now moved onto the next town near where our local test centre is, so, I still see her most days, she's no bother, she's harmless, bless her, well, today just topped it!!

We are stood waiting in traffic, and she walks up holding what looks like a baby in her arms. Because me and my pupil both know her, we were like, or bless her, look at her, she's got a baby doll but it looked so real!

She was carrying it in her arms, and cooing to it, and there's this old man and woman sat on a bench watching her. As she walked towards them, she flips the doll over, and grabs it by its legs, and starts swinging it about!!

Well, I thought this woman was going to have a heart attack!! They were both looking at her, and, just didn't know what to do!!

When we went by, I put my window down and said, "she has issues, it's a doll!" The woman said, "bloody hell, I didn't know what to do!!"

It is so sad for people like her, I really do hope she finds herself soon, and seeks help to enable her to have a better life, it's such a shame for her, bless her xx

Oh my God!! Why is it that when there are temporary traffic lights that vehicles actually park right up to them, so you can't get to the "stop here" sign? I understand they might live there, but even so, it's very inconsiderate, and if they are the censored ones, and you are trying to get up to them, and you say to your pupil, "just edge forward a bit love, the sensor hasn't got us" You have to explain about the sensors, and they are still stood there, and then, you just say, "for God sake, just do as I say! the sensor hasn't got us, just edge forward please, the sensor can't reach us because this dick head is parked here!!"

Ffs!! Just do it!! Haha!!

And, while I'm on one! Why do people reverse out of their driveways onto a major road, when there is clearly enough room for them to turn around in their drives!!

It is ridiculous, it's really, really, stupid!!

Is it just me, or our emergency vehicle sirens not as loud as they used to be? Why? and why don't they have the sirens on anymore??

They always seem to leave it until the last minute when there right behind you, and then, all of a sudden, the siren is on, and it's a mad panic to get out of the way, and, to be able to move to somewhere safe to let them by, then, they look at you, and all the cars, and it's like, well nobody could hear you!

Why can't you just put your sirens on before, so at least people can hear you, and prepare to move over in the road safely?

Yes, I do understand it is all to do with whereabouts they are, and even road markings, but, I like to hear a siren in enough time to prepare my pupils!!

Well, Oh my God! I have definitely seen health and safety at its finest today!!

A local farmer had a fork truck up to his top windows, and he was stood on the forks, cleaning them, I had to look twice!! Oh my God, how bad is that!! That is an absolute classic!!

We are approaching a train level crossing, and the lights come on for us to stop, there are 3 cars in front of us, the gates start to come down, and a motorbike overtakes us all, and whizzes in and out of the gates to get across!

If they had have got knocked off, that would have been it!! But, Think Bike, Think Biker and all that…

This was so funny today, we were slowing down for some traffic lights, and there are 2 lanes, and these 2 young lads, in a Corsa, went into the right-hand lane, and then transferred back into the left hand lane, just to get in front of us!

There was this old man in his car at the lights, next thing he's shaking his head, and chuntering away, so, when the lights changed to green, and the Corsa speeds off, next thing, this old lad gets his foot down, wheel spins his car away, and starts trying to keep up with these young lads!!

His face is an absolute picture because, he's proper grabbing the wheel, and leaning forward, it looked like he was tried to make his car go faster!! Me and my pupil just looked at each other cracked out laughing, bless him….

Chapter Seven

Aww, today I saw the absolute cutest thing ever!!

There was a tiny little bird in the middle of the road, and I said to my pupil, "ooh, watch this little bird, don't run it over, it only looks like a baby" next thing, this big bird swoops down, picks the baby bird up by the back of its neck, and flies off with it to safety!

We both just went, "Or Bless!" nature at its finest... it was amazing!

Nature always amazes me, they just instinctively know, don't they? Wow!

Last lesson of the day, and I'm a bit tired, and all that, excuses, excuses, so, you know this is going to be good if I'm making an excuse before telling you!! Haha!!

Coming up a country road, and we spot a zebra in the field, yes, a zebra!! Me and my pupil are both absolutely amazed, and we both go "wow! is that a zebra?"

On closer inspection, it's a horse, in a zebra blanket!! Ffs!! Oh, my days, I'm sure we are not the only ones that thought that either, surely, we can't be, can we??

Today I have a test with a girl who has taken her test 4 times before with another instructor, and, has even taken it in her own car, to see if it was any good, but it wasn't!

She was a bag of nerves! Even though she has taken some 'calms' tablets, so, just before the examiner comes out, I say, "right, listen to me lady, you can do this! you drive your own car all over, do you think your hubby would take you out with the kids in the car, if you weren't safe??"

This poor young girl who was with another instructor waiting for her test was just looking at me totally shocked!

I bet she thought I was a right cocky cow! Hahaha!

Anyway, the examiner comes out, shouts her name and I'm still like, "I'm telling you, you can do this!"

Anyway, a pass for my lovely girl it is!! Yyyyaaaayyyyy!! I'm so pleased for her! Its fab!!

You spend a lot of time in the car with your pupils, and you get to know them, and have a laugh, so, when this lovely young lad that I take driving, and you just know he wouldn't hurt a single soul, or, do anything bad to anybody, told me about the time he got put in isolation at the school, I was totally shocked by this, and said, "no way! I don't believe that what did you do??"

He was in a science lesson, and all the class was full of dick heads, who was messing about all the time!

Before the teacher came in, the 'bad lad' said, "right, we're all playing drop dead 12 o'clock" so, I started laughing, and said, "well what's that? I've never heard of that before!" So, he said, "well, basically, at 12 o'clock, we all drop dead!"

So, I'm totally laughing by this point, and I said, "what did you do?" So, he said, "well, the teacher was talking, and next thing it gets to 12 o'clock, and all the class just started falling to the floor, and there was only me left standing, so I'm stood there, thinking, shit! What do I do? do I have them have a go at me for being the only one left standing in the class, or, do I join in? So, I just fell to the floor like the rest of them!"

By this time, I can't breathe, I just had a vision of the teacher stood there, thinking what the hell is happening?? And, all the kids just falling to the floor! Ffs!! Haha!!

Anyway, the teacher left the room, and went and got the head of year, and, they all got separate isolations, spread over a few weeks!

I just said, "well I'm disappointed in you, I thought better of you!" He said, "I know, I didn't know what to do!!" haha!!

But secretly, I am just sssooooo glad that this was not out when my son was at school, because, I can assure you, he would have been the instigator of this...

How actually funny is that!! Omg!! Can you imagine the poor teacher!!!

I had a meeting with a trainee driving instructor today, he just wanted a bit of info on where to go, and what we do etc.

My first bit of advice was, expect the unexpected! Pupils do the most random shit!

It is always hard when you first set out, and you think it should be easy just to get 20 plus pupils, but my God it's hard!

He said, "it's OK Karen, I'll have all your pupils in the next couple of years!" I said, "you've no chance mate because I'm female!" He said, "what do you mean?" I said, "there's lots of people that choose a female driving instructor over a male one!" he said, "really?" "oh yes!"

Now, don't get me wrong, all the male driving instructors that I know, are extremely professional, but some girls just want a female instructor... and males come to that!!

It's just how it is!

I once had a 39 year old man come driving with me, and I said, "why the chuff are you coming driving with me, and not a man?" He said, "because I am always getting bollocked off our lass, so, if you bollock me, I'm used to it!" haha! What an absolute classic!!

Why do people stop for ambulances when they have no lights flashing?? This old man stopped at the roundabout nearly causing 3 crashes to let an ambulance pass, and they didn't have any blue lights on!! They were just driving on the road....

This job can be really shit for people paying you for their lessons. I really don't think people realise that it's how you earn a living, this is what pays, *your* bills.

So, this girl has her lesson, and then said, "is it okay to transfer it next week?" Well, what the chuff can you say to that? They have already had their lesson, so, I just said to her, "do you pay the week after at the ASDA, or do you pay on the day?" She just looked at me and said, "no!"

She then looked at me all confused, and she said, "or, I get it now, sorry" and just walked off... well, they don't do they? You've got to pay on the day anywhere else! What's the difference?

Nothing! That's what!

What is it with all these posh stupid lights and indicators?? You can't even proper see if there are indicating these days, I mean if you've got a bright light and then the indicators and a LED circle round like the buses that's ridiculous!!

They are there for a purpose not to just look nice! They are an important part of the vehicle!

I decided a long time ago, that I was not working Friday afternoons anymore, it's a crazy time of the week, everyone is rushing about, and quite frankly I can't cope!! Haha!!

But, today made me chuckle, we were on a country road with a tractor in front, then another learner, and a white van man. I looked in my mirror and his face was a picture! I bet he thought ffs, a tractor, and 2 learners! Happy Frigging Friday!! Haha!!

Well, this is just unreal what happened today! For the first time ever, I had a nose bleed in the car, whilst on a lesson!! Ffs!!!

As we were pulling into the car park to practice some Bay Parking, my eye started to itch, and then my nose, it felt like it was running. I went to wipe my nose and next thing, my hand was covered in blood! ffs!

I went into the boot to get some kitchen roll, and proceeded to conduct my lesson, whilst blood is pouring from my nose! I am glad that my pupil wasn't worried about the blood, she is wanting to be a nurse anyway when she leaves college, it's such a good job that she is, and not queezy about blood!!

But, according to my social media friends, I need to get to the doctors, but, what I don't say in public, is, that it might be because I have been picking my nose with my acrylics on!! Ffs!!

I had a first time past today, which is always good when this happens, but my pupil has hearing difficulties which I explained to the examiner beforehand. Luckily, she had already had experience of pupil with a hearing disability when she was an instructor. The pupil was totally deaf, so that made my pupil feel at ease.

It just adds to the pressure of taking your driving test even more when you have a disability, and you don't know the examiner.

In my experience, it is always good to be informative and the examiners deal with different people everyday, so, they are used to it.

Happy Yorkshire Day folks!!

Oh yes! Proud to be a Yorkshire Lass and all that!! Well, a Cas lass actually!!

Is it just my kid, that at 25 years old, still absolutely teases the life out of you!!

Rubbing my arms, and saying," Hey look at you, look at them muscles" and then messing my hair up saying, "what's up with you? it's only a joke!" Well clearly, I don't find it funny in the slightest do I?

But then again, it's all making memories...

Chapter Eight

I had a flashback today... to the day when we got chased by some teenagers on their bikes!! Ffs!!

We were driving in our local town centre, and there were a gang of kids on their bikes. Next thing, this lad pulls a wheelie, and I was like, "Oh my God! what is he doing?"

His pop fell out of his pocket, and we tried to miss it, but, actually ran over it!! It squirted all over the road, and this young lad is abusing us totally, shouting, "hey up, that's my pop, can't believe you just run over my pop, give me some money!!"

We just drove off, me and my pupil were laughing, next thing, we pulled up at some traffic lights, and the young lad was at the side of us with his mates!!

He was at the driver's side, banging on the window saying, "you owe me some money!" so, I put the window down a little bit and said, "you what?" He said, "you owe me some money, you ran over my pop!!" Anyway, I said to him, "you and your mates are on a busy main road, and, you shouldn't be pulling wheelies, it's not my fault that your pop fell out of your pocket, we didn't mean to run over it!!"

The next thing, he is proper up to my car, and saying," yes you did, it was her who was driving, she meant to do it!" I said, "hey up cock, do you think I'm that good that I can make my tyres go over a pop bottle?" The next thing, the lights changed to green, and off we go, and, I'm thinking, Thank God for that! The little shits!!

We both started laughing and I said, "bloody hell, getting abuse from 13 year olds!!" We then started to go down a very steep hill, and, as if the little shits are peddling like chuff behind us, I look ahead, and there's a level crossing, and I'm like, please, please, please, do not change!

I said to my pupil, "I hope them lights do not come on" my pupil said, "what if we have to stop at the level crossing and them buggers catch us up?" I said, "Megan love, it is not worth thinking about it!!"

Thank God the gates stayed up!! Because, if them lads had caught us up, I would have shit myself!!

Yyyaaaayyyyy!! It is the start of the football season, that can only mean one thing, the bets are on, and the accumulator has that one dead cert that lets him down!

So, let the swearing commence, and, bad mood Saturday's become the norm!!

Happy Days!!

Another first time pass today! check me out!!

It is always good for your street cred when this happens. Bang it on Social Media!! Oi oi....

We pull up at the side of the road. It's 10.45am, and I am just about to start explaining to my pupil what I want her to do, when we look up, and there is a man, and a woman, with a pushchair each, one has a baby in it, and the other a 2 year old.

There were walking down street with them, nothing out the ordinary there, except, they both had a can of lager in their hands and were drinking it, as they walked down the street! I said, "how bad is that?"

I mean, come on! At least do it behind closed doors.... some people just don't care!!

It's Ladies Day at Pontefract Races, a day out with the lady driving instructors. A few cheeky bets on the gee gees, and, a couple of drinks!!

We actually meet in 'spoons' got to keep up with the young ones and their sayings!! Haha!!

So, we are sat there taking selfies, and photos of each other like you do! And one of my friends said, "how do you take such a good selfie? I can't get my finger on the button at the bottom. It's too fat, and I can't keep my phone straight at the same time!"

"No, no, you press that button at the side where your volume button is" She said, "Do you?" I said, "Yes" she said, "well I did't know that! I don't think I've got one on my phone, show me"

"You just do it by pressing the button on the other side" She said, "you take it" I said, "no, you take it" So she said, "the button on the side and how?" There you go, a

Selfie! She said, "well I never!" She will end up being the selfie Queen, Hahaha.

So off we go to the races, we put some cash in a Kitty ,and pick a horse. Now these are the set rules. No form studying, just a nice name with the meaning, or, if we just like the colour!!

It was so funny at the races last year, we are all in our late 40s. There's things that us oldies just don't know how to do. So last year, it was the boomerang while taking photos!!

We ended up asking these young girls behind us how to do them, and then we said, "I bet them young girls are saying 'aww bless, do you think will be like that we get old?'" ffs! Haha!

Anyway, today we are reminiscing when my friend said, "how do you take selfies on an angle, do I put my finger on there?" I said, "wasn't you listening in spoons?" She said, "no, Why?" "It's that button on the side" She said, "What button?" so I showed her, she said, "can I take one on an angle now?" "Oh yes! who's the new selfie queen?" its competition time!!

Bless us! it is fun been this age though, never a dull moment, and always learning.

You are never too old, to learn something new everyday!

Jason's ex-boss, has three horses running at Pontefract today. We had a bet from the Kitty from the first race and it came last.

I text my son Sam, and he said, "mum get some money on that last race, on that horse of Blacky's" so, I had a tenner on it, and, it won!!.

Nice little 80 Quid win from Blacky's donkey! cheers mate!!

It was my Auntie Jackie's funeral today, such a lovely lady, beautiful inside and out and a lovely service and tributes and very kind words, and a very hard, but lovely speech from her grandson Sam.

When we went to the wake afterwards, I felt so alone, I really don't know what came over me! I think, it was been sat there, with my dad's brothers, their wives and kids, and it really hits home that I really am on my own.

All my cousins on my dad's side were there too, but I have no one. I am THE older person, I am that person that keeps the family together. I am that person that looks after everyone else, I am that person that they all come to, but who looks after me? who really has my back?

Okay Karen love, ffs! let's snap out of this....

I'm okay today, back to the Kazaa that everyone knows, taking control, and being in charge! Haha!

This morning I broke my nail, ffs! How much do acrylics hurt when they snap, need I need to get that fixed today!! It's like you're on a knife edge the rest of the day isn't it?

Shit! Is my nail okay? I hope I'm not going to rip the fucker completely off before I get it fixed! Should I put a plaster on? Or even more secure a bandage?? Fuck me!! Its only a nail!! Haha!!

On a lesson, and there's road works, and one side of the road is closed. We approached a car that is parked fully on the pavement. Obviously, no concern to us at all, until he begins to pull a wheelchair out of the back of the car.

He takes the cushion off the wheelchair, and then it starts rolling into the road! The man doesn't realise, I'm looking to the girl behind in the Audi in my mirror, as its heading right for her car, she edges further forward, and I'm like 'fuck!'

If my pupil rolls back here, we're into her!! I said to my pupil, "I've got the brake and clutch! Don't do anything!!"

My pupil said, "it's a good job there's no one in the chair, because that bloke doesn't even know it's in the road!!"

The next thing, he realises that the chair isn't there, looks round, sees it in the road, and he just laughs, gets it off the road, and back on to the pavement!!

Yeah, okay love, no worries, totally oblivious to the actions everyone around has taken, and then, can't even acknowledge the drivers who have to move!! Unbelievable!!

What is it with bus drivers and stopping at bus stops??

There was a parked vehicle on our side of the road, so we obviously stop, but there is also a bus stop slightly further down, on the opposite side, so the bus stops short of the actual stop, and blocks the road totally!!

Why??? All he needed to do was pull a bit further down, and the road would be accessible!! So, I just look at him in disbelief, and he just shrugs his shoulders, what an arse!! He knew exactly what he done!

Why do some people just choose to be knobs!! There is just no need!!

So today, in 10 years of doing this job, I have my first bump...

I was so scared!

Traffic was queuing on the other side of the road to me, and a car had left a gap. This taxi driver pulled out, and I knew he hadn't seen us because he looked up the road, straight passed us, and I said to my pupil, "shit! He hasn't seen us!!"

I grabbed the wheel and yanked the car towards the pavement. He eventually saw us, just as he was scraping the back of our car..

Obviously, my main concern was my pupil, so straight away, I asked her, "if she was okay?" and she said, "yes". I then got out of the car...

I took photos of both cars, and then went to the driver and asked for his details, but, all of a sudden, he couldn't speak any English, and didn't understand me! Now, I know full well that he can speak English, because he picked me up a few weeks previous, and he was chatting away... haha!!

Anyway, all he kept saying was "company car, company car" I was furious!! I said, "mate, I don't care if it's a company car or not, you've still got to give me your details and information!!"

He just sat there!! I just could not believe it!!

I rang my husband and him and my son came down, my son said to him, "here mate, she needs your details", and you got it, he just kept saying, "company car, company car"

Just then I looked up, and a car pulled up at the side and a lady got out of the back of the car that had bumped into mine with some carrier bags, and some painting in her hands! Ffs!! I was like, Oh no! Oh my God! There was someone in the back of the car!!

The next thing a man came to my car and said, "I am the owner of the taxi company, and I will pay you for your car, I will take your car now, and I will get it fixed!"

I said, "mate, you are not taking my car anywhere, I will get it fixed, and you will pay! Not, you take my car that you could get done anywhere, no I'm not having that!!"

He said, "okay okay!"

As if I'm just going to let him take my car somewhere, the dickhead!! Yeah, go on mate, just take it, do you want with it, and let me know when it's done!!

What was he even thinking!!! Haha!!

When we got home, my son said, "ffs mam, is that it? A few scratches!" I said, "fuck off! my car wasn't all scratched when I went out to work this morning!!" He said, "I was expecting airbags and all lot, not a few scratches and you having a do with the poor taxi driver!!" Whatever Sam!! Ha ha!

I know it wasn't really any thing massive, but you still get shook up don't you? AND, my car is still damaged!!

Jason's Nana Hilda passed away this morning aged 89.

Hilda was an old-fashioned kind of lady, called a Spade a Spade, and was quite outspoken! She didn't care if you liked what she said or not! Not in a bad way, but you know when your granny just doesn't give a shit what they say! Ha ha!

She welcomed me and Sam into her family and I will be eternally grateful for that.

I had a driving test this morning and honestly this lass is a mint driver!

I have known her all her life but she actually really does do my head in at times!!

She will be coming to a stop, really nice and gentle, then all of a sudden, she bangs on the brakes, so my head shoots forward, and she just laughs! I'm like, "ffs Jess!!"

Anyway, she had test, and she was following directions by the SAT NAV, and because she knew she had failed, she purposely missed the exit to come off at, and she decided that she will go past the exit, and take the examiner for a ride around the roundabout!!

When she told me, I just couldn't believe it! As if you would do something like that!!

Honestly, this job, haha!

You just couldn't make it up!!

We have a local running club round here, and also a get fit, couch to 5K run.

But, why is it that they just think they don't have to stop, and just run across the road?? They press the button at the pedestrian crossing and then just keep running…. So why press it in the first place?? Then your pupil is slamming on, just so they don't run them over!!

Quote of the day...

"Ooh Karen! Do you know what? I can drive much better today without my bra on!!"

Wtf!! Haha!! What has that even got to do with driving a car?? How does that even effect your driving?

I tell ya, you actually could not make it up!!

Bank Holiday Sunday!! Oi Oi!!

It is an absolute sweltering bank holiday for change!! The bank holiday weather is absolutely glorious!!

We decided we will go to Cas Vegas today, it's 'the lion fest' and they raise money for the Yorkshire air ambulance, not really into all that heavy music stuff, but, we thought we will give it a go, and obviously, for such a good cause too.

Ended up going up Ponte Carlo tonight after Cas Vegas for a few drinks, we saw some old friends in Ponte, and then met up with a couple of cousins, all in all, a good day!!

So, what should have been a nice chill out bank holiday in the sun, and we decided to take the decking up from the back garden, and basically, we were knackered!! But Jase kept on saying, "it needed doing love, and now it's done!!"

Or well then Jase, that's okay!!

Test passed today! So please for her, it will open up lots of job opportunities and promotions at work for her!! Onwards and upwards love!!

That is one of the really good things about this job, you can change someone's life for the better!! It's great when that happens, it makes you feel like you have THE best job in the world!

Chapter Nine

Just driving along, next thing there is a woman on a mobility scooter coming towards us on the wrong side of the road!

We slowed down, but she didn't!! I'm like, "ffs what is she doing?? Has she even seen us??" We have to swerve around her, and all she's doing is just looking at us!!

Now don't get me wrong, they really are an absolute godsend for people's freedom, and independence, but, some of them driving them, are just down right dangerous!!

4 days to go to my holiday in Zante and Sam is working away ffs!!

I won't see him for two weeks, I'm not happy, but bless him, at least he has a job!! I know, I know, I know how old he is and all that!! Haha!!

Today, we witnessed a 40 foot container doing a turn in the road at a junction where there's some traffic lights!!!

As if!!!

He just spun his truck around at the crossroads, and honestly, it was just absolutely ridiculous!!

All the traffic came to a standstill, as he was just manoeuvring this big fuck off 40 foot truck all around the crossroads!!

I tell ya, you really cannot make it up!!

My pupil that has had her test this morning said to me ages ago, "Karen, I really want to pass with no minors!!" Bloody hell….. I'm like, "Oh my God a pass is a pass!! Please, don't put yourself under so much pressure" but, to make it worse, her boyfriend passed first time with me, and so did one of her friends! Because she is so competitive, she really does want to pass first time, with no minors!! Ffs! No pressure on yourself then love!

Anyway, what did she go and do?? You got it, she passed first time with zero faults!! A clean sheet!!

You can't beat that then!!

I was so pleased for her and obviously she was absolutely buzzing but what pressure!!

Zante here we come….

We decided that we would fly from one of our local airports this time instead of Manchester, so Doncaster Sheffield Airport it is then!

The journey to the airport is only about half an hour, but due to my knowledge of the delightful A1, it is always busy and always gridlocked where it goes from the 3 lane A1M, to the 2 lane, A1, so, we set off pretty early to compensate for that.

Low and behold, was it busy? Er… no! sods law isn't it!!

We got to the airport that early, that the check in hadn't even opened!! Haha!!

The guy, said, "here just have a seat love it won't be long till they open!!"

How chilled out is that? Would that ever happen at a larger airport??

I think not…

So, it is mooch in the Duty Free time... oh yes! No holiday is complete without that is it??

I didn't bother taking my big tub of pro collagen elemis balm as I had planned to get a small tub in the duty free, like I'd seen in Birmingham earlier on in the year.

But, oh no! No Elemis!!!! I was devastated!!

I looked at the sales assistant and said, "what? You don't have any elemis?" She said, "we have this, which is really good"

Well, I'm not doubting it love, but, it is pro collagen? I mean, I don't want to be coming back from Greece looking 10 years older!! Haha!!

The flight to Zante was good, and whilst we on the transfer bus we saw Sam's friend outside the bar where he works.

We stayed at The Planet Hotel and Studios in Tsvilli, we were in the new building, and our room was amazing!!

We went and had a bite to eat and saw Sam's mate, he said, "I messaged Sam earlier because I wanted something from the duty free, but it was too late, you were already on the plane" so I said, "why, what did you want?" He said, "I wanted some 1 million aftershave" I said, "well, I have bought some for Sam because there was 20% off on the plane. So, you can have that love, and, I will buy some more"

I thought bloody hell, there better be some more on the plane going back, that was a Christmas present!! Haha!!

Well, the first day of our holiday and it is absolute bliss!! No kids because they are all back at school....

It is lovely and peaceful.. Oh, hang on, apart from one dickhead grandad!!

He was winding his little granddaughter up until she started crying and whinging, and then he was saying, "or I'm not having this, she's so bloody mornjey!!"

Bloody hell, hang on a minute mate, you're the reason she is whinging!! Ffs!!

Oh my, nice little trip to the shipwreck today!

Absolutely gorgeous blue green water amazing....

When we got off the boat to the shipwreck it was covered in graffiti!!! Why? Why on earth would you want to graffiti a shipwreck? Its beyond me...

I mean, maybe it is just me, but would you really go on a boat trip and get a spray can out of your beach bag, and write your name on a shipwreck??

Not my thing! Anyway, each to their own and all that!!

There were loads of people getting off the boat and going for a little swim, and I said to Jase, "ooh, come on, shall we go for a swim?" he said, "no Kaz! It's a bit too deep, and them steps area bit steep getting back up!"

Ffs! Jase! I'm not that old yet! I am sure I am capable!! What's with the protection all of a sudden!! Haha!!

We stop off for a nice little Gyros Kebab on the way back to the hotel, it was very nice! Yum yum!! Omg!! Absolutely Divine!

For some reason, the pool was really slippy, the first time me and Jase got in, we slipped, but apparently, so had everyone else! Well, that's okay then, we don't feel such a dick now!!

Well, this new family arrived, and I swear they had based themselves on the series, Little Britain!!

So, the first time he went to get in the pool, he slipped getting in but, instead of just carrying on, he made an absolute, massive, big deal about it!!

Everyone around the pool knew he had slipped, even if they didn't actually see him! It was hilarious!!

Even when this other guy in the pool went over to him and said, "it's okay mate, we've all slipped at first, its after you get off the steps, it's quite slippery!!"

Then, this guys sister comes down, and they are having a really loud conversation about who's getting a shower first, and how long it is going to take each of them, including mum and dad!! Ffs!!

But you know when you are trying not to look at them, but, you actually know everyone is!!

Then, this lad suddenly remembered by shouting, "oh no! I forget to tell you when we were talking about the shower, Dad needs a shave too!!" Omg!! Haha! So funny!!

Rain, rain, rain today!! That can only mean one thing… trip to the shop for some munchies!! Mmm…. Happy Days!! It always makes you feel better then!!

Not so sure if I wanted some Mary Juana chocolate!!! Omg…. As if they are selling that!!

I didn't have any by the way!! Just making an observation….haha!!

We stayed out until 4am!! Wtf!! Omg!! This is so NOT me!! I'm usually well in bed by then!!

And I argued with Jase about some random shit which I never ever do!! Must have been a bit of Dutch Courage and all that!! Haha!!

So, I am banned from the Harvey Wallbangers!!

The funny thing is, is that Jase will NOT argue back and I'm like, yap, yap, yap, so he gets off his stool and went to go to the room, so right cocky I said to him, "well, you're not going to get far are you? I've got the key!!" So there!!

So, he comes marching back, and said to me, "get off that fucking stool now, and get to the room!!" I thought who the fuck does he think he's talking to? So, I jumped off the stool and marched behind him, unlocked the door and we both dropped straight to sleep!! Ffs!!

The next morning, when we woke up at about 11… I was like, "are you alright love?" He said, "yeh, calmed down have you?" I said "yeh, bit too much to drink love, I love you Jase!" omg…

Well, tonight is our last night!! This week has flown by…

We go down to see Sam's mate, and we had a selfie, which Sam absolutely hates me doing! Ha ha!! Anyway, I put it on Facebook and his dad commented saying, "or thanks Karen, nice to see my son is okay!!" Haha!

I said to him, "here, your Dads commented on here, he's glad you're okay!

I got a text from Sam with a picture on it because he had fallen through the roof at work!! Omg!! How much do you worry when something like that happens and you're on holiday???

I was like "omg love, are you okay?" He said, "yeh, good job I grabbed the beam otherwise I would have been straight through the ceiling!!"

Bloody hell, as long as you're okay that's the main thing!!

Its hometime...

What a place Zante is...

We have loved every minute of it, we will definitely be back!

Our flight was delayed due to torrential rain at Palma Airport, which meant it was late landing back at Doncaster, and then obviously late getting the passengers over to Zante, hence us been delayed but, it can't be helped, Jase was on the flight radar tracking the plane coming in!!

What is it with frigging airports and bastard boarding cards???? Ffs!! I only wanted a bar of chocolate, you would have thought I was buying all the duty free how she created about the card. I had left them with Jase, so I thought 'fuck that' and just got one from the café outside!! It was cheaper anyway so winner, winner!!

I cannot wait to get home and see Sam and Alfie!!!

Why do you always get that one person on social media that is an absolute knob, and proper thinks they're funny with their comments, and you're like, or yeh, funny as fuck that mate!!

"Are you back off holiday? Didn't know you'd been away, haven't seen anything on Facebook!" Sarcastic twat!

I like to see other people's pictures, and where they have been, and loads of my friends always comment on mine too, so he can bollocks!!

Anyway, I posted this memes on my status...

"People talk about me behind my back, and I'm like, Damn, I got myself a fan club!" and the picture is of a woman with one finger over her mouth with a smug look on her face!! Haha!

Back to it!! Hi oh, hi oh, it's off to work I go...

Part of my tooth fell out today whilst I was chomping on some chewing gum!! Ffs!! That's what happens when you miss your check up! God repaying me for not going...

Dentist today... thank god!! My tooth is that sharp where its broke off, that it is cutting the inside of my mouth, I'm in agony!!

So, I can either have a crown for £286 to try and fill a massive hole but it might not work! Or she can just file it down and see what happens! Yeah, just file it down love for 22 quid, and we will take it from there! Haha!

Well, today we can finally lay Jason's nanna Hilda to rest.

Bless her, and the family waited until we had returned off holiday too.

The Vicar was fantastic! He was really light hearted, with a good sense of humour, a really good, lovely man!

And my Jason, carrying his Nanna's in with his family, bless him, such a lovely thing to do for her.

Yesterday I had a slight blood shot eye, nothing to worry about, or so I thought..

Omg, what do I look like today? Something out of the Exocist that's what!! Ffs!! Its Hilda's funeral too!!

No exaggeration, half of my eye is all red and looks like it is going to weep, its full of blood, bright red, bloody blood!!

Jase said, "Kaz, we will nip to A&E before the funeral" I said, "Jase, there is never no 'just nipping' to A&E!! I will see what it is like later"

I must say, I didn't look right cracking at the funeral, but at least I didn't need to go to A&E!!

The eye is better! Thank god! It can only get better to be fair, still looks scary, but better!!

Well, today the taxi company man finally rang me back, you remember the taxi driver...

I honestly thought he was trying to pull a fast one, but, he wasn't, he was genuine! I even phoned the actual taxi firm and was like, here, where's your boss? I need to speak to him!

It turns out, he was actually on holiday, that's why he hadn't been answering my calls! Haha!

Anyway, he has been and paid me my 80 quid so I'm happy!!

Chapter Ten

Absolute torrential rain today! Honestly, these windscreen wipers get on my nerves!!

We were driving along this road and there were loads of surface water, we was only going steady, obviously due to the conditions, when this big truck is coming in the opposite direction, he went through a massive pool of water, it absolutely covered the whole of our car and we couldn't see a thing!! Absolutely so scary…

We are contemplating a new kitchen, there isn't anything wrong with the one we've got really, but you know when you just 'want' one!!

Not sure if I can really be arsed with all the shit and hassle that goes with it though, but it will all be worth it in the end.

Anyway, I said to Jase, "I'm not sure if I can be arsed with all this kitchen shit, shall we just get the room reskimmed and book a holiday? After all, it is my 50th Birthday Year next year!!"

Jase is like, "yeh love, you only live once, get a holiday booked!!" well, you don't have to tell me that twice Jason love!

Jamaica here we come…

Nice early 8.10 test on a Saturday morning, that means a 7.10 start…. Who's idea was this? Ffs!!

But, he passes!! 3rd time like, but who cares? A pass is a pass!!

And, this also means he cannot pay me in bleeding 20p's again… ffs!! This is actually true, he once came out with a purse full of change to pay for his lesson, I just chucked it all in the bottom of my bag as there is no way my purse would have closed!!

I mean who even does that!

Just gets to the bottom of my hill, and this car proper cuts the corner at the top, and flies down the hill, it's only one of my ex pupils!!

So, I stopped and opened my window, I said, "cut corner a bit there didn't you cock?" He said, "well, all the people on the estate do it don't they? So why not?" I said, "well obviously I don't! but yes, they do, even though they do, that doesn't mean you have to does it now?" He then said, "of all the people to see that, it had to be you" haha!

Omg, today I was absolutely dying for a pee and the gates at the level crossing came down, no train though, just workmen… oh ffs! This is going to be a long wait. I am desperate for the toilet!!

That's the only thing with this job, no on site toilet!! Now, of course we can use the test centre through the day which is good, but I've finished now for the day, and I'm on my way home.. I am actually going to pee, please be quick with whatever you need to do!!

I'm not really sure what some people think of you, but anyway, pulls up outside this girl's house, and next door has a ghost figure hanging in the window that's as big as the actual window!

I wouldn't mind but Halloween is weeks away.. so, when my pupil got in the car I said, "bloody hell is it Halloween already?" So proper cocky, she said, "what do mean?" I said, "next door, look, a ghost in the window" she replied, "or shit Karen, sorry I thought you meant me, I thought I looked proper rough without my make up on, and you meant was I ready for Halloween!!" Omg!! No!! I didn't mean that!! Bloody hell... haha!!

Ffs!! I would never be that mean! Could you imagine? Been like that to one of your pupils!!

My pupil said to me today, "you know what Karen, It's mad what you tell your driving instructor isn't it? The stuff I actually tell you is crazy! You're like my own personal counsellor" I said, "I know love, what gets said in the car, stays in the car!" And, it absolutely does..

Some people tell you their whole life history, or they will get in the car and say, "I need to talk to you"

It's re-skimming the walls day... I am so excited!! The smell of the plaster, and the lovely smooth walls... I cannot wait!!

All the wallpaper is off, curtains down, curtains poles taken off, it's a nightmare!! And it makes it even worse when Jason takes my tools!!

I have a drawer that I have had since I was on my own, that has all my basic tools in, but Jase just 'borrows' them, but never puts them back!!

Honestly, it makes me so angry, just put the fucker back, its simple!! Jase thinks I'm some kind of absolute mad compulsive psychopath, who's obsessed with having her own screwdriver, but they are mine, not his, and he needs to respect that, and put the fuckers back, then there would be no need for an outburst would there? End of!! Simple!!

So, we are up at the crack of dawn, moving the settee, and omg! What a scruffy, mucky cow!! There's absolute thick dust everywhere, half bitten chews of Alfie's, bloody screwed up betting slips that Sam has just chucked behind the corner bit of the settee, ffs! Why not just chuck them in the bin?

It's a good job the plasterer wasn't early, I need to have a good clean up!! He would have wondered what kind of shit hole he had walked into!!

Oh my! How actually nice are freshly plastered walls?? Lovely and smooth and that smell, mmmm…. A kind of clean, mucky smell, well if that is ever a smell!! Haha!!

I told the plasterer that I would clean up it was okay, ffs!! How actually stupid of me was it to say that!! It was never fucking ending!!

It was dust upon dust upon dust, right fine shitty little dust upon dust!! It took me a lifetime! Well, a couple of hours, but it felt like a bastard lifetime! I was knackered!! Ffs! Never again!

By the time I had put all the furniture back, and all on my own might I add, I was absolutely shattered! Back ache, shoulder pain, legs aching where I'd pushed the settee back with my leg, and to top it all it was my friends 50th Birthday Party but I just couldn't go, I was physically shattered!!

Well, today I was expecting to get up to lovely dried out walls, and still have a lovely clean house! Oh no!! The walls were still wet, and the dust had settled again… lovely fine fantastic fucking dust! Oh my! Let the cleaning commence, again… I'm not really in the mood to be clean, clean, cleaning on a Sunday morning!!!

Oh my! Still aching from the weekend!! But, I need to crack on...

We pulled up at a junction and it's a good job that we were only going slow as a woman on a mobility scooter flew past us with a child on her knee!! Me and my pupil just looked at each other quite shocked, and just burst out laughing!!

How actually dangerous was that though???

She was absolutely whizzing about, but she was going that fast that she nearly hit the green communications box, and had to swerve around it!! Ffs!!

The poor kid nearly fell off!! It was only early morning, surely, she couldn't be pissed at that time! Could she?? Haha!!

If there is one thing that really pisses me off, its starting work early, but then having a gap and then having to go back out!!

It is so frustrating!!

I work late on a Monday, but I finished at 3 but then had to go back out at 6!! Ffs!! Absolutely does my head in!! I know its not anyone's fault with work and that, but even so, it still pisses me off!!

Drivers on mobile phones!!!!

Today this young girl that was behind us and was too busy looking at her phone, that she nearly crashed into us!! I was absolutely furious!!

She was looking down, and I could see her in my rear view mirror, and she just looked up, just in time to brake!!!

Anyway, we pulled over and let her pass, I'm not having her behind me, get her in front where I can see what she's doing!!

Omg! This has got to be one of the funniest things ever!!!

So, its 7.15pm and I went to our local supermarket to do our weekly shop, as I pulled into the car park there was a car in front of me and there were 3 parking spaces near the front.

The car in front pulls into the middle of the 3 spaces, but closer to the line on the left hand side, than the right, so because there was more space in the right hand parking bay I decided to park in that one.

As I'm pulling into the bay, he flings his door open, so I acknowledged him to continue getting out of his car and that I would wait.

Well, he starts looking around the car park, putting his hand above his head like he's gesturing, looking for something, and I'm just sat there just looking at him thinking what's with this dick head, just get your bags, shut your door and get your shopping done! Ffs!!

Then, real slow, he starts getting his bags off the back seat and keeps looking at me, so I thought, I aren't playing games dick head, I'm too busy for this shit!

I reversed back out of the space, and went into another one, because he was blatantly taking the piss and quite frankly, I was just not in the mood.

When I got out of my car, he was staring at me, so I thought fuck it! I'll ask him, 'what's up?' Haha like you do!!

So, bear in mind I am raging, I said, "what up? What you looking at?" He said, "well, there's all these spaces here and you park in that one next to me!" I said, "yeah and??" He said, "well why, why would you do that?" But, he's not *'talking'* to me when he's saying this, he's practically *'singing'* it to me!!

Now looking back, it was really funny, but at the time, this wound me up even more!!

I said, "well, for 1, I can actually park on this car park where I want! And 2, why have you parked in the middle bay of 3?" So, in his fucking singing voice again, ffs!! He sings, "oh, I can park wherever I want, its nothing to do with you!"

I said, "yes, I know you can! And, so can I! And, if you had parked correctly in the bay in the first place, I could have gone to the other side of you, but because your parking is crap, then I couldn't!! Prick!!"

So, he sings again, "I cannot understand why there is ALL these spaces, and YOU choose THAT one!"

I said, "you know what, just fuck off cos you're doing my head in!!" haha!!

I thought if I see you in there, I'll ram you with my trolley you dick!!

And, I was that wound up walking round, I didn't get half my shopping!! You know when you're that mad that you just can't think straight!! That is so bad!!!

Why, oh why, do people have to drive so close behind you?? And, it is even more frustrating when they have kids in the car!! It is absolutely disgusting, it really annoys me! How on earth would they be able to stop safely when they are so close??

Another kid complaint....

This kid ran to the end of the drive near a busy main road, whilst Granny Annie is putting a coat on another kid!!

Just get hold of their hands ffs!! Keep them under control, AND keep them safe!! It's not hard is it, to make sure that your kids are safe near a busy main road!

But, I suppose if I had said anything, it would have been the usual, 'they wouldn't have gone on the road, they know not to'

No, but what *if* they slip or fall? It's all about 'what if?' Safety first...

It's Women's Rugby League Grand Final Day!!

Castleford Tigers Ladies played Leeds Rhinos at St.Helens tonight, excellent advert for women's rugby league, just such a shame that the result didn't go Cas's way, but at least they got to the final and I am super proud of every single one of them!!

It's a far cry from when I first started playing in the late 80's when it was totally amateur, and the women's game was born!!

I feel proud to been part of that era, because to be fair, I was shit! and these women these days are total athletes, and an absolute credit to themselves, and the game!

My dad used to love coming to watch me and my sister play, and then tell his workmates all about the game on the Monday when he returned to work!!

I broke my ankle and had to have it pinned that's why I stopped playing!! I will never forget it! We were playing Halifax, and we was right on our try line, and thinking I was Jimmy Lowes, I thought right, if I get to acting half back, (even though I was a prop), I thought, I'm over here!

I've seen Jimmy Lowes do it all the time, I'll send the dummy out, then go over the line for a try the other way!

Yeah, alright Karen love, course you will!!

This chuffing lass knew exactly what I was going to do, and she was on me! My foot stayed where it was in the muddy field, and my body went down! Omg!! The Pain!!

My Dad took me to A&E, and I ended up having to have it pinned, hence I never played again....

But, that doesn't stop my passion for the game and for the growth of the Women's Rugby League!!

Well, today was a bit of a sad day in our area, as 4 cooling towers got blown up in a controlled exercise. This had been a huge employment industry in previous years.

I saw the first cooling tower come down in the controlled explosion, which was to see how the towers would fall, and exactly what would happen, there were a lot of people out watching and it felt quite eery, just stood there, all in silence, just waiting...

We were stood on a hill at the top of a field and had a really good view of the cooling towers, everyone was waiting with anticipation.

There is a big motorway network near the Power Station too, and the traffic had to be stopped on there for safety reasons!

We noticed that an eery silence, fell all of a sudden, this was because the police had stopped the traffic on all the roads and the motorways around the area, and you just couldn't believe how silent it fell without the sound of the traffic.

Everyone was waiting and you could hear whispers of 'ooh, the traffics stopped it won't be long'... next thing, a siren sounded... and it fell deadly silent...

Whilst we are stood there in absolute silence waiting, a flare was set off by the company to make sure that no birds or animals were around the towers, everyone jumped out of their skins and you could hear whispers of 'ffs!' Then people laughing!!

Next thing, a roaring bang and one by one the towers fell.... gasps filled the air, and everyone was amazed at how the towers fell, caving into the middle of their own tower, dust all around.

Such a sad time, but what an amazing thing to see! I have always wanted to see this happen rather than just on the television, and now I have.

Everyone was having a bit of a joke about it, saying, 'oh no! How will we know we're nearly home now, if there's no cooling towers to look out for!!'

You always have that one icon don't you, that lets you know you're nearly home when you see it, and, ours was the cooling towers...

Oh why, oh why, do people open their car doors onto the main road to put their kids in!!! It makes me so mad!!

But, what makes it worse, is the fact that they then look at you like it's your fault!!

What's wrong with getting in on the driver's side, and climbing in the back of the car to fasten them in?

This is what I used to do years ago, but people just don't care anymore, or have no common sense, I don't actually know which... or, maybe it's a kind of fuck it, the traffic will have to stop, kind of attitude! Who knows...

Oh My God!! How actually embarrassing is this?? You certainly could NOT make this up!! Here goes...

Jase has decided he wants to get a new car, which to be fair, he has always had my old driving instructor car, so I can't blame him.

I said to him, "I will ring the insurance company, and see how much the insurance will be". I went upstairs and got the insurance documents and gave them a call.

I got through to the company and gave them my policy number, he said, "ooh, I'm sorry but you don't have any insurance with us", I said, "ooh, don't I?" He said, "no, you did last year, but you didn't renew.." So, slack arse me, said, "well, who am I with then?" He said, "I don't know, but it's not us!"

Haha!! Omfg, how embarrassing!! I said, "ooh, I'm really sorry to bother you, er thanks, bye..."

I had only got the chuffing policy schedule out and not the certificate of motor insurance!!!

Anyway, when I put the phone down, me and Jase just burst out laughing, and I was like wtf!! And you know when you just sit there and stare at each other because you can't believe it! But also, I said to Jase, "it's not funny, because I actually don't know who we are with!!" Haha!!

We both just sat there looking at each other and then laughing, and I'm like, "yeh Jase, but it's serious is this, because I actually don't know who we are with!!"

So again, we just burst out laughing...

Finally, after absolutely racking my brain, I said, "Sheila's, that's who we are with! I remember now, I did it online that's why I didn't have a paper certificate!!" So, Jase is like, "yeah love, Sheila's that's it.."

As if I asked him at the other insurance company who I was with!! ffs!! Haha!!

I pulled up outside my pupils house and switched the engine off. I'm going through the lesson plan with her and then we go to prepare to move off.

She goes to start the engine and it just goes, click, click, click.. So, I said, "is you're foot down fully on the clutch?" She said, "yes." "Ooh that's strange then, why isn't the car starting?"

I got in the driving seat and it did the same for me, click, click, click! Wtf!!

Next thing, car disabled!! What?? What's happening here??

I rang the breakdown company, and a guy comes out to me, and it's the battery! A dead battery!

I said to the guy," well it has been okay, it's not been struggling to start or anything", he said, "no, they don't have to, they can just die.". "Or okay!"

So, 135 quid later and we are back on the road!!

Chapter Eleven

We were turning right out of this wide, one way junction, and there was a car in front that was just smack in the middle, so as we are approaching, I said to my pupil, "just watch this car because I don't know which way they are going, it doesn't look like they are convinced themselves!!"

We pulled up at the side of her and she is on her phone eating an apple!! Ffs!! It's not a picnic area love!!

So, there is traffic either side of her, whilst she's debating where she's going!!

I tell ya, you just couldn't make it up!!

You always have that one pupil that brightens your day....

This woman is THE best!!

You just do not know what is going to come out of her mouth... and today was an absolute classic!!

She said, "I'm mating George today (her white miniature schnauzer) with another schnauzer." I said, "aww, bless him!" She said, "I know!!" Then she said, "so, I've bathed him, and brushed him, and made him smell really nice for his date later on!!" I said, "what? Why?" She said, "well, let's face it, you wouldn't go with anyone smelly, would you? She needs to fancy him!!"

Omfg!! Honestly bless her!! Haha!!

This job is no good at all for posture and weight, and to be fair I'm struggling with both...

I went for a massage tonight, and honestly, she pressed on my shoulder and it was like concrete!! It killed!! More than one session for me then I think...

Those beautiful, fresh, silky new plastered walls have been painted today... looks amazeballs!! But, I'm absolutely knackered, and too tight to pay anyone to paint it for me!!

The colour is Cancun... now the paint is on the wall, I can only imagine, it's called that because of the colour of the beach??

It's like a nice, light beige, with a hint of grey, just like a beautiful fresh clean beach, it looks amazing! So light, so clean, so fresh... beautiful...

When I went to pick my pupil up his mam was stood at the door, so I said, "hiya, are you okay?" She said, "well I will be when I've de-fuzzed!"

De-fuzzed??

So, I said, "de-fuzzed??" She said, "yeah, you know when you shave all the fuzz off your legs and under your arms and that?" I said, "well, I've never heard it called that before!!" De-fuzzed!! Ffs!!

When her son gets in the car, he starts telling me about this girl that he fancies at Uni, so I said, "well, why don't you ask her out?" He said, "because she's just come out of a relationship with a girl" so I said, "oh, so she's gay?"

He said, "no, she's not gay", I said, "oh, is she bisexual then?" He said, "no, she's Pan?" I said, "Pan?" He said, "yeah, you know Pansexual?"

I said, "no, never heard of it!"

He said, "are you kidding?" I said, "no! Is this just a word that you young ones have made up?" He said, "no Karen, it's not made up it a proper word!"

Well , well, well, you learn something new every day in this job!

He continued...

"She's not hetro or bi, she's pan!!"

"Okay, so what does 'Pan' mean then?"

He said, "well basically, she will just be with anyone who she fancies male or female.."

"okay then, so isn't that Bi?"

"No, it's not Karen! Bisexuals are attracted to both, and Pansexuals are just attracted to the 'person' regardless of their gender!"

Oh, okay then...

It is times like this, when you actually realise, you're getting old...

Oh, and another realisation of you getting old, is getting extremely excited about finding a lampshade that actually matches your curtains perfectly!

Priceless.. Happy Days... Haha!!

I went to pick my pupil up who's mum has a shop in our local market, so obviously I parked up at side of the market. There is a car also parked up with a man in, so I parked in front of the man's car.

Next thing, this guy in a van pulls up at the side of me, bear in mind I have a roofbox on my car with my name on, and just stares at me... I looked at him, and he just looked away, so I thought, or he must just be waiting for someone!

I looked up again and he was still staring at me... wtf!! I put my window down and said, "orate mate?" He said, "well, I'm wanting to get in there love, are you loading like?"

"Well, er, no... I'm waiting for my pupil who's mum works in the market, but it's okay I will move."

But then, because I was really pissed off and I think he only asked me to move because I was a woman, and he didn't ask the man behind to move, I said to him, "have you asked him to move like?"

He just stared at me!

Yep, your staring right at me, because, you know you haven't! I will just pick on this woman, parked here and all that.. Knob!!!

Anyway, my pupil came out, and off we went!!

College kids, sorry... young adults, sorry.... No fucking kids!!!

Honestly, one of the local colleges near us has a quite narrow pavement along the main road and the students just walk out onto the road, they don't care, it's like the vehicles are invisible!! Ffs!!

And speaking of college, the residents that live there are a pain too!!

They moan if you're parked there, and dirty look you, and they are always reporting it to the council or getting the local parking wardens down!!

Now, yeah, fair point, if the college had just appeared there, but it has been a school for as long as I can remember, and I'm proper old, so obviously it was some kind of educational establishment when they bought the house??

#justsaying and all that...

Oh my! This is one of my absolute bug bares....

So, people go to let you out at a junction, and you say to your pupil, "right, they're letting us out, look, we can go." But, obviously your pupil needs to get to the 'bite' and make sure they don't stall, and then double check its clear, but then, by this time, the person that was going to let you out has got pissed off of waiting for you, and they set off before you!!

Ffs!!

WE ARE A LEARNER DRIVER!!

Give us time….

Don't go to let us out if you're not prepared to wait!!

And even more so, when it's you're right of way, Dick Head!!

Early morning lesson and we just set off when a Fire Engine comes round the corner, blue lights and all, just as we overtaking some parked vehicles, shit!!

I slammed on my brake, bangs it into reverse, and reverses back into the space!! Phew!!

Fireman acknowledges, all sorted…

My pupil was still in shock! I was too quick for him to even think!!

I am actually getting worse at not been able to get the petrol pump money exact!! I always like to round it up to the pound, and not have any extra pennies!!

You can guarantee it is always 1p over, and it really pisses me off!!

When I went into the shop to pay, I said to the cashier, "is there something wrong with them pumps? I'm always a penny over, you'd have thought I was a bit more experienced now and could get it bang on!"

She said, "no love it's you!!" Haha!! Cheers love!!

Off to Blackpool today to see a comedian! Can't wait! It has been years since we've been to Blackpool!!

Omg! Stayed in the Football Club Hotel, wow! I would highly recommend!!

Gets checked in, and then it's out, out, Baby!!

Omg, it is absolutely freezing and so windy!! But then again, we are in Blackpool and as my mum always used to say when it was windy, 'it's like bloody Blackpool front here!!' Haha!

First pub is The Castle, oi oi!! Has this pub even changed in all these years?? Couldn't really hear the songs for the DJ talking all the time, telling really bad jokes, and laughing really loud at his own jokes... go on lad!!

Next stop, Flagship!!

Played some right music in here!! Loved it!! Nothing like a good old Saturday afternoon dance!! Oh hi... go on lass... who cares? We're in Blackpool!!

We could not find anywhere to eat!! I know it's the Blackpool Illuminations, but ffs its heaving!!

We end up in an all you can eat Chinese buffet, and both me and Jase both saying, "right we won't eat a lot because it's only early!" Yeh right! That never happens though does it? You're always stuffed when you come out!! Greedy fat pigs in all you can eat Chinese buffet!! Haha!!

Walks to the end of the North Pier, omfg!! How actually cold and windy is it?? I am absolutely freezing...

We couldn't wait to get in the venue to see the comedian, but, ffs! It was absolutely freezing in there, don't get me wrong, amazing place, and obviously back in the day, it would have been one of the best!! But Jesus, it is cold!!

The comedian comes on stage and 1 minute later, people start fighting in the audience!! Ffs!! Haha!! Wtf!!!

All the audience is shouting, 'Fight, Fight, Fight!' It was like been back at school!!

The comedian just sat down on the edge of the stage, and he said, "I knew it, I just fucking knew I should never of agreed to a Halloween weekend in Blackpool when you lot's been out on the piss all afternoon..."

The support act then came on at the interval, no one was listening to him, so in the end, he said, "Fuck it! I'm done!" And walked off the stage!! Haha! Ffs! What's going on here like!!

The comedian comes back out for the second spot and they start fighting again!! Honestly, you just couldn't make this shit up!!

And I'm not naming the comedian, because I was bitterly disappointed with the performance, but then again, it was spoilt by a couple of idiots!!

But anyway, walks back up the freezing pier!! Calls in a pub for a swift drink, then gets Fish and Chips to take back to the hotel.

Well, all I can say is, 'you can take the lass out of Cas and all that' but… sat on the bed, in your hotel room, eating Fish and Chips out of the tray and a bottle of lager!!

Happy Fucking Days!!

Advent Calenders…

Right, so for kids these days it's all about the chocolate!!

My pupil was talking about them and getting proper excited and I was like, "it's a chocolate, one small chocolate a day!! Is that so exciting??" Maybe it's just me…

When I was a kid you used to look forward to getting up on a morning, and seeing what picture was behind the window!

Candle, Mistletoe, Holly, Santa, Elf the list is endless, but one thing you did know, was that behind the big double window at 24 would be Mary and Joseph with baby Jesus!! Everytime!! But that didn't make you any less excited!!

None of that these days! Just a chuffing little cheap chocolate, but then again, if you're like my son, you just eat them all at once and bollocks to opening it one day a time!!

That is exactly why, I don't buy them anymore!! Haha!!

Bloody hell, on a lesson today and this woman had fallen over with 2 dogs and she was leaning on the fence. I stopped and asked if she was okay? And she was like, "yes love, I'm okay, you're alright love, don't worry!"

I obviously knew she wasn't, so I got out of the car and I said, "it's okay love, you're alright", so I got hold of the dogs for her whilst she got back off the fence, and her shoe had also come off, then the dog's harness was coming off too!

I waited until she had done that, and I said, "are you sure you're okay love, I can wait with you, it's okay". She said, "no love, I am okay, but thankyou for stopping and waiting with me to make sure I was okay."

Aww, bless her! Good deed for the day done!

Where the frigging hell does all these nails and screws come from that you get in your tyres???

I have a nail in both my front and rear nearside tyres!! Ffs!! That's all I need!! Oh, and I have a test tomorrow at 9.07 so I should pick her up at 8.10 but the garage doesn't open until 8... gonna be cutting that a bit fine Kazza!!

Goes to the garage mega early, and luckily there is no damage to the tyres, they just took them out and away we go!!

So, I'm in a right mad rush to get to my pupil because of her test, I pulled into her street and there's a chuffing van blocking the road!! Ffs!!

The worse thing about it is, is that if he had pulled a foot further forward, I could have got by because there was a little layby, but no, the dick head just stopped smack outside the house with no consideration for anyone else!!

He looked up and said, I'll be 2 minutes love! So, I acknowledged him, and sat patiently waiting....

Next thing, he goes back into the back of the van and starts getting some more furniture out, then starts taking all the wrapping off!! I'm like ffs! I've got a test!! The woman who's house it was, was really apologetic, bless her!!

Anyway, I had to ring my pupil and ask her to walk down the street because I couldn't get to her!!

When I got out of the car to let her in, this guy was looking at me and I said, "it's alright mate, she's only got her test soon, don't mind us!" then I muttered, 'fucking dick' he just looked at me, as much to think, bloody hell, alright love! Haha!!

Then to top it all she failed for going too close to a parked vehicle!! Ffs!!

Chapter Twelve

With a fairly new starter today, and she is worried about what lane she is in, and because she was in a car accident a few months ago, she's worried that she's not going to be able to stop safely, and in time!!

So, we are behind a van that is in the lane to go straight ahead, which is what we want to do. Suddenly, he changes lanes, and swerve's across into the other lane, which takes you onto the motorway!

My pupil panics, and just spins the wheel round to follow him!! I'm like oh, Shit!!

It was one of those incidents where you're like, ooohhh, what do I do for the best here?? Quick! Think!

If I pull the wheel back, is that going to be more dangerous than letting us carry on? I just don't know!!

I checked over my right shoulder straightaway to make sure we wasn't going to crash into anyone with changing lanes, and then decided what would be best!!

I looked in front and all I could see was us getting closer and closer to the crash barrier!! Ffs!! Think! Think!

I couldn't get the wheel back round in time to get us back on track where we needed to be, so we had to carry on in the lane to the bastard motorway!!

I still had to grab the wheel and push it right round to the right, otherwise we would have hit the kerb!!!

So, even though by this point, my heart is pounding out of chest and beating in my throat, but, I still have to get us to safety!!

There is no way I can take her on the motorway, she would absolutely shit herself!! And, the criteria is, that they should be a competent driver which she isn't, so the motorway is definitely not an option!!

I indicate right, look over my right shoulder and navigate us across 3 lanes to get us back on track!! Ffs!!

All in a day's work and all that!! Haha!!

I looked at my pupil and she was just sat there just looking blank!! She was probably thinking, wow, wtf has just happened here!!

I then said, "don't worry hun, we're safe! Are you okay?" she said, "yeah, yeah Karen, I'm good thanks!" yeah, like fuck you are love, but we will crack on... haha!!

Happy Halloween!!

I have a test today, and she's been absolutely smashing it! Only getting a few minors here and there on her mock tests, I am confident she will pass, but who knows...

Before we had got out of her estate she had already stalled twice, and then stalled getting out of her estate onto the main road... she said, "ffs! What's wrong with me?" I said, "it's okay huuni, just pre-test nerves!"

We got to the test centre and we practiced a reverse bay park, and she turned the wheel the wrong way every time... ffs!! 'Which way do you want the back of your car to go?' Just turn the wheel that way... simples... anyway she finally cracked it and we moved off.

Next little practice manoeuvre, reverse parallel park... ffs! That was the same! Turning the wheel the wrong way!! I said, "right love, listen to what I'm telling you... just stop pissing about with the wheel now, and just turn the wheel whichever way you want the back end of the car to go"

Anyway, she goes out on test and passes first time with 5 minors! I am so happy for her!!

I said, "what manoeuvre did you do?" she said, "parallel park, and guess what? I totally fucked it up, but all I could hear in my head was you saying, Holly! Stop pissing about with your wheel now and just turn it the way you want the car to go! And I did it!"

Well, there you go then love, all sorted, haha! I did feel a bit bad been a bit cocky, but hey ho! It worked!!

Obviously, we can't be friends with the examiners, but you can still have a laugh can't you!

An examiner comes back in off test and myself and another instructor said, "morning, are you okay?" he said, "what's up," I said, "nothing, I'm just happy!" he replied, "why? Because it's Halloween??" Boom boom! Haha! Nice one Kev!! I suppose I walked straight into that one didn't I...

You know, this job isn't just about teaching people to drive, you get a sense of what this age group of kids are like!

They are all at that age when they are still at college, not really knowing what to do in the future, carry on education by going to university, get an apprenticeship and hope that they will have a job at the end of it after been on a shit wage for 2 years, or, just try and get a job, but then where does their experience come from... its hard...

So, today we have no hot water!! We have heating, but no hot water!! But then, my delightful husband mended it, so I cancelled the engineer... well done Jase!

We have a business meeting in Leeds today for the Flight Simulator, and that means I'm happy because we can go Christmas shopping, can't we!!

I might as well as have a treat and take my 'Love to Shop' vouchers with me, all 300 quids worth of them!! Happy Days!!

After, a very successful meeting in Leeds, we hit the shops!!

Now, let us bear in mind here that my husband is the tightest person in the world, and is a nightmare to shop with!! I will say to him, "ooh, do you like this?" and he will look at the price tag and say, "ooh no, that's too expensive" and puts it back!!

Well, oh no, not today... it was like fucking supermarket sweep!! He didn't even look at any of the prices, he got 2 of the same jeans, yes 2! And I'm just there thinking, 'fuck me will I even have enough vouchers!!'

He actually spent 250 quids worth of MY bastard vouchers, I only got 300!! Ffs!!

Then, he had the chuffing cheek to say, "didn't think it would that much Kaz!" so I said, "oh, well how much did you think it would be? Did you even look at any of the prices?" so he just started laughing and I said,"'well I know you didn't! and, there's fuck all left for anyone else now"

Obviously, I kept reminding him about this for the rest of the day! Like you do!! Haha!!

How actually funny is it setting up an Echo Dot??

So, we are doing voice recognition, and I'm speaking but Jase had set it up on his phone, so when Alexa said, 'is that Jason?' he answered, "yes!" I'm like, "no! no it's not it's Karen!" ffs!! Honestly!! I mean why do we even think Alexa is real anyway!! Haha!!

Well, we finally get it set up, and just started asking random stuff, like you do!! Then I asked Alexa, "what she had been doing?" she replied, "just looking at the clouds!" haha! Then Jase asked her, and she said, "I've been learning new things!" haha! Go on lass...

So, it turns out, that we don't any hot water after all....

If the heating is on, we have hot water, if it's not, then we don't!! back on line it is, to get the engineer out...

This evening, we have very nearly crashed!!

My pupil was approaching some traffic lights that were on red, but they then changed to green, so she changed down into second gear, but then thought, ooh you know what? I'm not actually sure what gear I am in!

So, she looks down, but keeps her foot on the brake, and this car behind is luckily turning right and just misses the back end of our car... ffs!! Absolutely, shit myself!!

Fireworks...

So, what is it with everyone going on about them!! Now personally I like fireworks, and my dog isn't scared of them either, and I do see where people are coming from, but this is my take on it..

Fireworks should only be let off on Bonfire Night, and then we wouldn't have all this shit if it was, just 1 night but depending on when the 5th falls! It shouldn't actually be spread over 2 weeks because that is absolutely ridiculous!!

Back in the day, when we were kids, bonfire night was on the 5th except when it was on a Sunday and then it was on the Monday! End of! Simple!

Back at the Slimming Club tonight...

How's the diet going then Kaz?

To be honest, falling apart like a cadbury's flake mate... haha!

How much fun is it when of your pupils has the same birthday as you? Well, I will tell you how much shall I? None! And why is that? Because he keeps reminding me that I will be 50 and he will be 18... that's why!!

50 chuffing years old... ffs!!

I mean come on, 50 years old, how the hell did that happen? Don't get me wrong I'm glad it has, I mean I could have popped my clogs a long time ago, so yeah, I'm happy!!

You know when something just pops into your head when you see someone, and you can't stop laughing? Well, that happened to me today...

A driving instructor was telling me years ago about this pupil that he had, and she had failed her driving test a few times, and she also owed him £20.

She then started driving with another instructor, but, still owed him this 20 quid.

Anyway, it turns out that she started working at this factory where this pupil works who is now driving with this instructor.

So, this ex-pupil, had been telling his current pupil, about not passing her test and all that, and that she had her test booked for this Saturday. She told the instructor and he said, "well, you know why she hasn't passed don't you?" so she said, "no why?" he said, "because she still owes me 20 quid and the examiners know this!"

For the record, The Driving Examiners knew no such thing, it was a joke!

But anyway, this current pupil goes to work and tells his ex-pupil this.

When the driving instructor gets in from work there's an envelope with £20 in it, apologising for not giving him it sooner... the instructor is totally oblivious to this happening and just thinks, oi oi! About time!!

Saturday comes, and low and behold his ex-pupil passes!! Omfg!! How funny is that!!

Absolute pure coincidence, but he has 20 quid back, and she passes her test!! Happy Days!!

Now, you just couldn't make that up!

Love this Social Media Quote:

'Rock bottom will teach you lessons that mountain tops never will'

How actually true is that?

There are times in our lives when we really are at rock bottom, but then, how much do you actually appreciate what you've got, and know actually hard life is! Doesn't it actually make you work harder so you're never there again!!

If everything is rosy in your life, then how on earth do you learn anything?

Just learn to appreciate everything in your life, because it all can all be taken away in an instant...

Well, for the first time in my 10 years as a driving instructor a car has hit me from behind...

We were approaching a roundabout and was going to go when a van came flying round and we had to stop! We were just looking to see when the next gap was to go, when a car went into the back of us!!

I looked in my rear view mirror, and the guy behind was like a rabbit in headlights!! He just sat there staring...

Obviously, my first concern was my pupil! I turned straightaway to him and asked him if he was 'okay', to which he replied, "yes".

I then got out of the car to go to the driver behind. He was so apologetic and sorry. He said, "omg, are you okay? I'm so sorry, I thought you'd gone, I didn't realise you had stopped".

I said, "yeah we are both fine, thankyou, and we had to stop because the red van was flying round", he said, "yeh, yeh of course".

We checked over both our cars, and to be fair my little fiesta was in better shape than his Merc! His car was quite badly smashed on the front, where as, my car just had a few cracks on the bumper!

What an absolute ball ache it is with the insurance companies though...

For me, it is just the absolute hassle of it all, that quite frankly, I just don't have time for! In the end, I decided I would get the car done myself and stand the 80 quid cost rather than all the hassle!!

We drove off, and I'm still quite shook up, and it just pisses me off so much as to why other road users just drive so fucking close up behind you!! Just stay back..

I love my Social Media memories...

This one came up today and it was so funny...

when your pupil stalls the car at the junction, and there's a load of vehicles coming up and down the road, and you're thinking chuffing hell, we're going to be here all day!

Then, suddenly, the lollipop man comes into the middle of the road to stop the traffic for her!!

No-one waiting to cross, he just did it for us!! We pulled out of the junction carefully and slowly and I acknowledge him... ffs!! Ha ha ha!!

I'm a bit confused lately to the lack of sirens on emergency vehicles!

We were approaching some traffic lights, and next thing there's an ambulance with the blue lights on that pulls out of a junction, we have to slam all on, and then the car on the opposite side of the road stops too, but blocks the road, the ambulance driver is having a right go at me telling me to move and arms up in air because the road is blocked!

Well, for 1, if you had your siren on, we would have been looking all around and more prepared to stop safely, and 2, more than likely the vehicle opposite me would have too! And 3, just for the record, cut the attitude!! Ffs!!

Now, don't get me wrong they were clearly attending an emergency, but to just 'appear' out of the junction isn't good, and when you have a learner in the car you have to plan a bit...

My nephew's fiancé rang me today to say that they are pulling their wedding forward because his Grandma is terminally ill.

I am devastated.

After crying on the phone to my nephew and his fiancé, I'm like, right then! All guns blazing, we have a wedding to prepare for...

I am wedding dress shopping... I saw a dress online and it was absolutely, gorgeous, I have ordered it! Fingers crossed it looks as stunning on me, as it does on the model...

Chapter Thirteen

Jason is taking someone flying, in a real plane today! He flies from Doncaster Sheffield Airport, as that's not too far away from where we live.

He rings me and I thought, ooh, I bet he's going to tell me he's on his way home and tell me all about the flying.

Oh no... he's only gone and locked his car keys in the boot!! Ffs!! How do you even manage that? Well, I'll tell you how, shall I?

You open the boot, just with the boot key, you don't open the actual cars doors, and then, you put the keys down in the boot, then you forget they are there, and you shut the boot!

That is how!!

You then go to open the car door, and find it is locked, you then look through the window into the boot, and then you see your keys staring back at you… ffs!! What a dick!!

He said, "Kaz, you're going to have to come through with the spare keys!" I'm like, "are you been serious??" He said, "yes love".

I set off to the airport and then he rings me and said, "get your foot down love, I need to get back to the simulator!!!" cheeky get! It's not me, that's locked my bastard keys in the car! I'll be there, when I'm there…

When I got near the airport, I pulled over and rang him to see whereabouts he was. I kept him on hands free, and this is how the conversation went… get ready…

"Kaz, you need to be where that hanger is"

"I can't see a hanger, I'm near that hotel, am I near you?"

He's like, "well, erm"

I said, "ffs Jason, stop going round the houses, am I, or aren't !?"

So, I obviously cannot stop and pull over anywhere here, because I'm in a controlled area, and I've been round and round and round this fucking roundabout 6 times! Bastard airport security will be coming soon! The dick!!

I finally found him! Allaleujah!! I got out of the car, opened his car with the spare set, he got his keys out of the boot, and we set off back...

I am that fucking mad when I'm driving back out of the airport, that I take the wrong turning, and haven't got a fucking clue where I'm going, but I thought, you know what, I'm not turning back round, he can fuck off, I'll get lost first!! Like you do! Haha!!

I see a sign for the M62 and I'm like aahh, that's nice, I know where I am now...

I finally get home and relax...

After chilling this afternoon, I take Alfie out for a walk. I bump into this couple who have a new little puppy, I'm talking to them about their puppy, and the next thing, Alfie is pissing up my leg!! Ffs!! That's all I need! About right for today that!!

Well, today has shocked me...

I noticed that a manhole near us had water around it for the past few weeks, and usually one of my neighbours is on the ball with things like this, so I thought I better report it to the water company.

I reported it at 7am, I got a call at 1pm to ask which manhole it was (er, that with the fucking water round it!) and it was fixed at 2pm!! Blocked drain, all sorted!!

Well Done The Water People !! I am impressed!!

Jase decided today that we would take the laminate floor up in the living room and dining room ready to put the new down... yip-fucking-eeh!!

Well, we got quite a bit done, really cracked on! Just putting the furniture back and I went to pick the settee up, and I forgot about the big fixture on the side, that links the settee to the corner seat, and I rip off my acrylic.... Aarrggghhhh!! Fuck, Fuck, Fuck!! I daren't even look!! I'm just grabbing the end of my finger, hoping the pain will go away, and hoping I still have a finger!! Ffs!!

I finally dare to look... its broke off over my actual finger, I feel sick...

Anyway, I get a plaster on it, and my only worry now is that how am I going to get these soaked off safely? Do I keep one finger out? What happens to that nail? Ooh, it's not worth thinking about...

Why is it, that people don't press the button at the pedestrian crossings, but then get the monk on when the traffic starts going and just look up at the traffic lights and then the car!! Ffs!! Press the bastard button!! That's what it's there for!! To stop the traffic!!

Just press the button love and the green man will come on and then you can cross safely... yyyaaayyyy!!!!

Ooh, how bad does your nail actually throb, and hurt? #Acrylics...

Please tell me it's not just me that has 50 thousand wires, at the back of their television? Where the fuck, do they all come from? We have a television and sky, that's it! What even are all these cables for? I'm confused!! Haha!!

Well, I bet I sort the bastards out, again...

I have a test today, and, well, let's say, that the lesson before was not his best...

We are sat in the waiting room and he said, "do you think I will pass Karen?" I said, "well yeah, just don't be a dick head and do something stupid!"

Guess What?? He only went and PASSED!!!! Well Done!!

So, why is it that when I go to do something lately it all goes tits up!!!

I bought Jase a private plate for his car, but we haven't received the log book yet, so, I rang the DVLA and the guy from the garage hasn't even sent it off yet, so I cannot do it!! Ffs!!

We finally have the log book... yyyaayyy!! I can't wait to get them plates on!!

Here we go! Kazza at her finest... ffs!! Get ready...

Put the plate on by doing it online, easy peasy...

Oh no...

Apparently, I've put the wrong postcode in! What? Like I don't know where I live?? Ffs!! So, after 3 attempts, I'm locked out, and I need to get a code from the DVLA!!

I rang the DVLA and the guy was really nice, and he said, "it's okay our system has been down this morning, it might be that"

My phone then starts bleeping and someone else is trying to get in touch with me, I look to see who it is, put my phone back to ear and the bleeding thing cuts off... ffs!!

I rang the DVLA back and she said, "oh yes, you've put the wrong postcode in" really?? Like, I don't know where I live!! I think I do love!! So, I said to her, "well, I've lived here for over 20 years love, I think I know my own postcode!" she said, "yes, I am aware of that, but it's the postcode of the company you bought the retention certificate from, not yours!" ffs!! "oh, okay, thanks for your help, I get it..."

What a tit I am!! Haha!! Anyway, all done...

On a lesson today and as we approached a junction on our left, a truck driver was waiting to come out, and as we passed, he was waving his hand about out of the window and shouted, "ffs! Just let me out!!" erm, why? It's our right of way!!

But then again, its Friday isn't it?? Ffs!! Friday!!

I absolutely hate driving about on a Friday!! Everybody is in a mad rush, flying about like dickheads!! It does my head in!!

It has just come up on my memories about Christmas Tree Baubles not been straight and people having OCD about them, well, that's me!! Bloody hell, when Sam was little and you're like, "ooh, let's put the tree up" but then the baubles are just randomly placed all over and you're like ffs! My OCD is in overdrive! I can't wait until he goes to bed to sort it out!! Haha!!

I remember once, I went to my mam's and she had blu tacked all her Christmas cards onto the door, omfg!! They were just chucked on!! You've never seen anything like it!!

One slanting to the left, the one next to it slanting to the right, then a gap and then a vertical one instead of a horizontal, ffs!! Honestly, I just looked at it, and, I could feel my whole body shudder, and my fingers curl!!

I took every single card off the door, and then placed them back on in an orderly manner, all correct and present, all nice and neat, all the same way, all is good...

My mam was like, there's summat wrong with you... haha!!

It has been all over social media about Organ Donations, which I am 100% all for, and this is how our conversation about it went with Sam...

"Right, if I die, they can have anything except my eyes!"

"why can't they have your eyes? What if someone desperately needs them?"

"Well, I'm sorry but they can't, I still need to see what you lot are doing whilst I'm up there!"

"what makes you think you're going to heaven? You might go to hell"

"well, I don't think that's going to happen, do you? You know I'm Miss Goody Two Shoes"

"Or, yeah Mam, I forgot about that!"

Haha!!

New Television day today!! Yippee!! Oh no!! that can only mean one thing!! Yes, you know it, the 50 thousand cables at the back will have to be sorted...

Now, I know I'm exaggerating, but come on, where do all them chuffing cables come from? They're not even plugged in to anything, so why are they there?? I'm confused!!

I mean, do they just breed? And what's happened when they were unplugged? Was it just a, 'ah fuck it, I'll leave it there moment!'

So, we get the television up and running, and I'm like, 'right, hang on, cables!! What's that one for? Do we need it? If not, bin it!!'

Ooh, that's nice, a nice clean area, with no extra cables at the back of the television, I'm happy....

My husband just does not get recycling whatsoever!!

It absolutely frustrates the life out of me!!

It does my head in beyond believe!!

Every recycling bin day, I have to check it, to make sure he hasn't just put some random shit in it!!

To be fair, he's done quite well lately, but I still check!! Well, today it's a good job I did!!

There is a poo bag on the top, yes, a bastard shit bag of Alfie's!! As if they would take that!!

So, last night, he took Alfie out, but instead of just walking an extra 2 foot to the waste bin down the drive, he just flung it in the recycling at the end of the drive!! What a dick!!

It is amazing what my pupils come out with!!

This girl has failed her theory 7 times, and as we were coming up a hill, there was a parked car on our side, and, she didn't stop for the approaching car, so I said to her,

"you need to stop and let them pass!"

"no, I don't!"

"Yes, you do! Why don't you?"

"because I'm going uphill"

"what? What's that got to do with it?"

"Well, because if I'm going uphill it's my right of way!!"

"is it chuff!! It's got nothing to do with that at all, the obstruction is still on your side regardless of the road!"

So, she come out with this absolute classic!

"well, my mate Ben, said that if you're going uphill it's your right of way!"

I said, "well, I think he's winding you up there love!! Why has he said that? Because he can't do hill starts??" Ffs!! Haha!

One of the worst things that has happened to me in my job, is this guy, that was very close up behind me, and I ended up getting out of the car to him…

One of my pupils was approaching a junction and to be fair, she was going really, really, slow, but she is learning after all… as we approached the junction to turn left, he nearly went into the back of us!!

I was furious, so I just put my hand up through the seats, as much to say, "What are you doing???"

Well, he spun the car round after us, and was that close to us that he was nearly actually touching the back of my car!!

My pupil was absolutely shitting herself and if I'm going to be honest, so was I…

I said to my pupil, "we need to pull over, he's dangerous!" she said, "I know Karen, I'm a bit scared!" I said, "it's okay love, don't worry, we will just pull over and see what happens".

We indicated left to pull over, and ensuring that my pupil didn't brake, and that I would do it from my side with my dual controls, because I just wasn't sure what he would do…

We managed to pull over safely, but, so did he…

I sat there thinking, shit!! What am I going to do... Do I get out of the car to him? Do we just sit here? Or do we just drive off and risk another chase?

Fuck it! Who does he actually think he is? Has he just seen a women's name on the roofbox and decided, it's only a woman? Is he a bully to women?

Shit! I'm out of the car, bounding towards him, my heart beating out of my chest, up my neck and into my head...

Well, he is the smallest fucking man, sorry, prick, I've seen in my life, and let's be honest I'm not the smallest of women, I bet he shit himself!! Haha! Good! The fucking bullying arsehole!!

I was marching towards him and I said, "who the fuck do you think you are? Why was you so close to us and following us?" he said, "fucking you! Gesturing that I'm a wanker!"

"What?"

"yes, you did"

"no, I didn't"

"I fucking saw you"

By this time, he is actually shoulder barging me, and, trying to get to my pupil, and I'm like there's no fucking chance of that mate!

So, whilst he's right in my face, well, tits actually, he's that fucking small!! We continued our argument...

"she's a fucking learner! So, what if she is a bit slower going around the corner, what do you think that big fuck off red L is on the top of my car? It's not there for the fucking laugh is it!"

"I don't give a fuck, she shouldn't be going that slow, it's ridiculous!"

"she's fucking learning! Wasn't you a learner once?"

"yes, but not like that!"

"Anyway, fuck off back in your car there is absolutely no need whatsoever for your behaviour!"

"I'm not going anywhere until I've sorted this!"

"sorted fucking what? There is NOTHING to sort!"

By this time, he is angry as fuck, and I am quite worried that this is going to escalate...

I am just stood there like a fucking bouncer, not really knowing what his next move is going to be, but one thing I do know, is that he is not getting anywhere near my pupil!! No chance!!

He then said, "I work for a newspaper and I bet I write an article about you!"

"whao!! Do you now? Well, well, well... you know what then sweetheart, you crack on cocka, because I cannot wait to read that!!"

"oh, I fucking will love! I'm absolutely sick to death of all these fucking driving instructors round here, they do my fucking head in!"

"really?"

"yes, really!"

"well, I can't wait to read that!! And don't forget to write about your road rage towards me and my pupil will you? I am sure your editor will be extremely proud of your actions today!"

"oh, I fucking will"

"good!"

He then glances back to his car and I can see someone sat in the back, and I thought shit! He's driving like that and he's got someone in the back of the car!

I then said, "well I tell you what, to say you was in a massive rush, flying about, and nearly crashing into us, you've just wasted some right time here mate!"

Wait for this, he said..... "yes, I know! I have my pregnant, (yes PREGNANT!) girlfriend in the back of the car and we're in a rush to get home!"

I said, "PREG... NANT GIRL... friend.... Well, what a fucking boyfriend you are!! You're driving about like a fucking dick, and your PREGNANT girlfriend is in the car?? Well, you know what love? After this today, then she should fucking dump you because that's absolutely disgusting behaviour!! Ffs!! Make sure you mention that in your big fuck off article too!! I am sure that will make even better reading!! Best seller that cock!!"

He said, "I'm fucking sick of your attitude! I don't know who you think you are?"

"chuffing hell, that's rich coming from you mate!"

He then tries to open my door to get to my pupil and I'm like, "hey up, I've told you now, fuck off back in your car and fuck off now.."

He said, "I am, and you'll know about it!"

"Yeah, course I will Billy Big Bollocks!! You crack on, and write your article, I mean let's face it, you're not exactly fucking Fleet Street are you? More like our local paper, so anyway, let me know when it's done hun, and then I can absolutely rip you to bits with my reply!"

He replied, 'fuck off!' got in his car and sped off....

Fucking hell, never, ever, has anything like that happened before, and even though I'm acting hard as fuck, I actually shit myself!

But, you know when it's one of them situations where you're like, you know what, I just CANNOT back down now no matter what! If I had have done, he would have absolutely wiped the floor with me, and that was never going to happen...

Anyway, the next day, I'm telling my pupil about it, we pull up at some temporary traffic lights, I looked in my rear-view mirror, and who the fuck is there? HIM!! Ffs!!

I just stared at him through my mirror and he just turned away... this road that we were going onto is a national speed limit country road! I was quite worried in case he started been a dick head again!

I told my pupil that if anything did happen, I would take control...

Nothing at all happened!! He kept his distance behind us!!

Now, I can only think that once he got home, he probably thought, SHIT! What just happened? Or, his pregnant girlfriend had a right go at him!!

And, just for the record, he never wrote the article...

Chapter Fourteen

I have actually just saved a massive accident from happening, with my quick thinking...

We were on the slip road to join the A1, we checked our mirrors and there was a car in the slip road behind us, and then there was a van on the actual A1, we indicated, the van moved over to the right-hand lane to let us into the left hand lane, perfect...

Not really, the car behind us came straight out of the slip road, straight across the left hand lane, and straight into the right hand lane!! Ffs!! She clearly did not check her mirrors at all!!

She didn't even get any speed up at all, and, was just plodding along at the side of us, totally oblivious to the van that has just had to slam on the brakes and is still gaining on her!

I could see the van driver and he was gripping the steering wheel, his whole body stiff and I could tell, he was braking, his hardest!

Okay? So, what do I do? He's clearly not going to be able to stop safely, so, he's either going to swerve and hit us, or go straight into the back of her!!

Quick.... Think!!!!!

I looked over my left shoulder and pulled us over into the hard shoulder for the safety of us all... I then looked over my right shoulder, just as the van squeezed between both our vehicles!

The look of relief on the van drivers face was unreal, he put his thumbs up, and mimed, 'thankyou!!'

My pupil was really shook up about it all, but, I encouraged her to carry on.

Now I'm against all abuse to anyone, but, when this driver got out of his van to this woman at the roundabout, I was glad!! She needed to know what had just happened, because, she really was totally oblivious to it all...

Right! That's it! These Acrylics are doing my head in!! I've just broke another one changing the bed!! Ffs!!

I've just bit them off, I know you shouldn't, and they look a twat! But tough!! I've had enough.. and now my hands look short and stumpy!!

How actually fuming am I today??

Remember that Dyson hairdryer? Well, how could you forget! I went on about it for that long!! Haha!

Well, today, it is a TSV on the shopping channel!! I am livid!! And, it's 60 quid cheaper!!! The presenters point blank said that it would never be a TSV... when I emailed them about it, their reply was that they always seek to get the best possible deal for their customers...

Well, this is a classic!

Me to my pupil, "what you doing later today then?"

"dying my hair"

"what colour"

"what colour do you think?"

"I don't know?"

"come on Karen, its Christmas! What colour do you think?"

"erm, red?"

"nearly, Red and Green!"

"RED and GREEN!!" wtf!!

"yeah, Christmas innit!"

"oh yeah, silly me"

Tonight we should have gone to one of my pupils 18th Birthday Party but Jase was ill..

Well, I say pupil, I have grown up with his parents and know all of his family quite well. This lad has a form of celebral palsy, but, omg! What an inspiration this kid is...

He is the most, happy, go lucky person you could wish to meet!

He started having driving lessons with another instructor in a specially adapted automatic car, but his parents didn't feel like he was getting anywhere with his instructor.

I was in Lloret De Mar, for the Cas game against Catalan, now bear in mind, I'd had a few too many beers, so I'm under the influence of alcohol, when his parents ask me if I will take him driving in his own car, and I'm like, "yeah, course I will, no probs love!"

It was only the next day when I thought, Shit!! What have I done?? There are no dual controls in his car!! No safety net!!'

But, you know what? We have laughed so much, it's been an absolute pleasure!!

Don't get me wrong, we've had some near misses along the way too, and me screaming, BRAKE, BRAKE, BBRRRRRAAAAKKKKKE!!!!! And of course, my feet pressing into the footwell when there is fuck all there! Haha!

He once leant forward to see if anything was coming to his left, and banged his head on the adaptation on his steering wheel and the wipers and the indicators come on!! We were crying with laughing it was so funny!! Bless him!! He's the Best!!

He has also always dreamt of playing at Cas Tigers ground, and is actually Cas's biggest fan!! But, due to his disability he hasn't been able to play Rugby League, but, a recently a league has been formed called the PDRL and he's actually played at the Cas ground and scored a try!! Go On Lad!!!

He is such a happy person, always smiling, he doesn't let anything get him down, or get in his way of what he wants to achieve!!

A True Inspiration.

Honestly, my husband does my head in with this log burner! He must be the thickest fucker going when it comes to this bastard fire!!

It is actual common sense that a fire needs oxygen to light!! He just chucks some firelighters on, chucks the wood on, chucks some coal on, and then expects it to boom…. Ffs!!

1st December and the Christmas Tree is up!!! I don't even know how people can wait until 12 days before, I can't wait!!

When we were kids, we always had a real tree because my Mum and Dad had their own greengrocers and we used to sell real trees. I can always remember, that, every year, my Dad would say, "here, this will do!" and it was always the shittiest tree, and my Mum would be so unhappy about it and my Dad would say, "well, no-one is going to buy that are they? They will want a good tree! We can't have the best one, we need to have what won't sell!"

Mums words were always, "Tight Twat!" ha ha ha!! But, good memories!!

When I'm putting our Christmas Tree up, I always remember when Sam was little, and my mum was putting the tree with us, and he nearly fell on to the tree!

You know what it's like when the kids are helping you, and they always want to reach onto the bloody top!!

Well, that's what Sam did, he was reaching onto the top whilst stood on the arm of the settee and lost his balance!! Ffs!!

It was total slow motion... my Mum just managed to grab the back of his pyjama top and stop him from actually falling into the tree!! He turned around and went, "woah! That was close mummy!!" it certainly was Sammy Boy!! Haha!

The last couple of years we've had an artificial tree after having a real tree for the last 5 years. I honestly don't know which is the worst, fannying about putting the artificial one together, or, taking the real one down with all the needles all over, and the headache of disposing of it...

Anyway, either way its Christmas!! And, I am buzzing!! Oi Oi!!

Oooohhh, here we go again! Now with the Hair wrap!! Haha!!

Yes, I know, we had a big debate about the Hair Dryer, but this wrap does look amazing....

Anyway, big curler it is for 50 quid in the sale!

Sam's been looking at a private number plate for his car, but the one he has seen is for a 10 plate or over, and his car is a 59 plate, so he can't have that one!!

We've both been looking at different plates, but he has his heart set on this one, which to be fair is quite cool…

After much consideration, I have decided that I will change my car and get a new one, and Sam can have my car because it's over a 10 plate. I would have been changing my car soon anyway so we can do that!

Bloody Kids!!

So, I have been looking for another car and, I'm taking the plunge and getting a petrol one, not diesel….

Now, yeah, maybe this is no big deal for an experienced driver, but I am worried that my pupils will struggle with the 'bite' and that it won't be as good on the clutch as a diesel, and that my pupils will be scared and worried.. but, on the plus side, it is well cheaper!!!

Might use a bit more petrol than diesel, but we will see…

New Car Day!! Yyyyaaayyyy!!

I am excited about getting this car, but on the other hand, it's petrol... ah well, too late now!

I call to the garage, and meet the guy who is taking the dual controls out of my old car, and putting them in the new one. Now that is something I can't do without, my brake and clutch on my side!!

I drive the car away, and I am well pleased with it! It's lovely!

My pupils absolutely love my new car!! I told them all I was getting a new car the previous week, just didn't mention that it was petrol until they got into the new car!! Haha!!

Sam is also happy with his new car!! The only thing is, is that now he is pestering the life out of me to get his new plate on! Ffs!! Give me chance!!

So, because Sam is going on and on and on about it, I took the plate off my car, which is also a personalised plate, and put Sam's on. As soon as I took the plate off online, I thought, shit! I've not got a retention certificate number! I thought, ah well, I will ring them on Monday and sort it.

Sam is absolutely buzzing with his number plate and one his friends took a photo of the car, and sent it to him on snapchat, saying, "please tell me this is you, and this is your number plate, it's sick!" (sick, apparently meaning good) haha!!

I rang the DVLA and I can't just do it over the phone, what an absolute ball ache this is going to be!!

So, I have to wait until the log book comes back for Sam's car, and my car, then I need to take Sam's number plate back off (he was mega pissed off with me for that) And then, I need to take my number plate off, to then put Sam's on!! Ffs!!

These number plates are having my life!! But, lesson learnt, and it won't happen again I can tell you, I'm stressed to fuck with it all!!

It is all good now! We all have our private plates on our cars, and we are all happy!! At last!!

Another classic Karen alert…

I bought a new watch from the shopping channel, it is amazing, bling, bling, bling! I love it!! The only thing is, it is too big, so me and Jase look to take the links out and can't really see where they come out, but you know when you just daren't mess about with it, incase you break it, so, I said to Jase, "leave it! I will take it to the watch shop in the market and let him do it!"

I take the watch to the guy and ask him if he can make the watch smaller, he looks at the watch, looks at me, unclips a link, and said, "is that okay?" I said, "or, yeah, is that it? I could have done that myself!" he said, "yeah, I know, that'll be 50 quid!!" I said, "I orate, course it is cock!" we both just started laughing, and I said to him, "honestly love, you want to try been me! I amaze myself sometimes!" he said, "I can imagine" haha!!

Ffs!! I am so thick at times, it's unreal!!

Anyway, no charge!

Just dropped Sam and his mate off to go out drinking and I'm in Jase's car, now he obviously forgets what my job is, and he does my head in saying, "Kaz, be careful in my car" ffs! I can drive Jason!!

Anyway, Sam's saying, "mam, get your foot down, stop sticking to speed limits" and I'm saying, "Sam! Shut up! It's 30 for a reason!" so he said, "well there's no roof box on this car, get your foot down love!" "no Sam! I'm not!" then his friends saying, "Karen, you used to tell me off all the time for speeding so don't do it, or I'm reporting you to the DVSA!"

"shut up Danny or we will never get there with her slow driving"

"She's a driving instructor Sam, she can't"

"she can"

"she can't, because I will report her"

Christ it's like they're 10 again!!

Next thing Danny said, "did you check them mirrors then Karen? Mirrors…. Signal…. Manoeuvre… don't forget Karen, I won't be happy with you! You need to make it obvious, not just moving your eyes!"

"Danny, shut the fuck up"

"No Sam!"

"Mam, please put your foot down because you're both getting on my nerves!"

They get out of the car and Sam is like, "thank fuck, I'm stressed to fuck! I wish Jase had picked us up instead! See you later Mam, I love you!"

"See you later love, I love you too, have a good night!"

"Drive safely back Karen, don't forget to check them mirrors and watch your speed"

"I will Danny, thanks.."

"Ffs Danny! Shut up!"

"okay Sam"

I bet they have a good night… haha!!

Asking Alexa how many days it is Christmas is the best... I'm like a big kid!! Not long to wait now!!

Election...

Eeh, it's all fun and games isn't it? It's just absolutely taken over everything hasn't it? And everyone on social media, all of a sudden becomes a bastard politician!! Oi Oi!! You look on your news feed, and you're, like, ooh, hey up! Here we go...

My favourite post was the one where someone put a picture on saying:

"If Jeremey Corbyn gets in, he will reduce Freddos back to 10p!" haha!

Oh my.... A 2 metre long Pig in Blanket!! mmmmmm!! That's going in the freezer till Crimbo let me tell ya!! I was ssoooo tempted to cook it this Sunday with the dinner!! But, then again, it would take the novelty off the Christmas Dinner then wouldn't it?

Bloody good job we didn't have that pig in blanket I can't get another anywhere!!

It's our Lady Driving Instructors Christmas get together!

We just stay local and for the past 2 years we've just gone to a small cocktail bar that does Afternoon Teas.

Well, last year for me was well, just me! That's all I can say about it!

When we are arranging it, the Consensus is that we will have a couple of drinks before and meet about 2pm. Because there isn't another driving instructor near me, I make my own way there. Now, for some weird, and wonderful, strange reason only known to me, I go to our local Wetherspoons, which is at the other end of the town to where we are having our afternoon tea.

I walk in, on my own, go to the bar, get a drink, and look to find them. Oh! There's no-one else here! That's strange! I circle the pub, (twice), still can't see them!

I ring my friend and she said, "ooh, we are sat near the door," I look to the door no-one there! I ring her again, and said, "I've got a drink, I'm at the door," she said, "no, you're not! I'm stood at the door," I said, "I am, I'm here", she said, "what at Minx?"

"Minx? No! Wetherspoons!"

"Why are you at Wetherspoons?"

"Well, isn't that where we are meeting?"

"No! Minx! We are waiting for you!"

"Or fuck! I'll be 5 minutes!"

Honestly, why did I even think we was meeting there? What is wrong with me? Haha!

Anyway, I make the trek to the other end of town, to a round of applause from the girls!! Ffs!!

All together there is 11 of us, and we are all on one long table, but, there isn't enough room for all the teas, so we share, which to be fair has really pissed me off!!

So, we're all like, 'ooh, do want that? Can I have that?' and in my head I'm like, ffs! We've paid for a tea each and I'm having to ask someone if I can that! Well of course I fucking can! I've paid for it!

Then, when we had finished and had the sweet course too, they brought 5 more teas out!! Wtf!!

Now, this is backwards arse round if you ask me! We had all 'made do' with what was there, and to top it all there was a lovely cream slice on our stand that I clearly had my eye on.. bang! Someone took it!! Ffs! I was fuming!! Haha!

We ended the night with a few drinks in the local pubs, and a good chat and a catch up! It was lovely! We don't get together enough these days!!

You know sometimes, we can all get caught up in the 'buying' and 'spending' at Christmas time, and this I came across on my news feed, basically sums it up!

'What do you get your mum for Christmas when she deserves £2 billion and a mansion overlooking the Caribbean, but all you can afford is a packet of skittles'

Well, I'll tell you what you get her! Nothing! Because if you can't afford it, then that's fine! And as you get older, honestly, the quality time spent with your kids, is very few and far between, and memories, and time, are worth far more than anything materialistic!!

#Makingmemories and all that...

If there is one post that circles that makes me gip, it is the pineapple on pizza one! Yep! That's right! Straight in the BIN!!

I can eat pineapple, but not hot, and definitely not on a Pizza!!

Chapter Fifteen

So, back to the election! Round here, is mostly labour, and today we had a supposed, handwritten letter, from my 'neighbour Val' about not voting for the conservatives, but to vote labour!

Now for one, I don't have a neighbour called Val, and 2 they were all photocopied! And what made it even more comical was that my friends in the towns around me got the same letter, just with a name change! Ffs!

So, mine was Val, we had Sandra, Julie and Sarah... haha!!

The Apprentice!

This is my favourite time when they absolutely rip to bits their business plans! I mean, let's face it, some of them you think really? But then others, you're like, ooh yeh! I get that plan! Go on!!

It is Voting Day!!

I have been to cast my vote, and to be fair, I didn't really have to think too much about who I was voting for!

I don't actually think that anyone could have predicted the huge majority, but let's just hope it's all for the best...

This is so many of my pupils..

How to Parallel Park

　　1.　Park somewhere else

Ffs! Classic!!

Well, Today the Rugby League World was rocked by the news, that a young ex rugby league player has motor neurone disease.

This is a devastating illness, and my heart goes out to them all, and everyone else who has, or who is battling this, or knows someone who is.

I watched the interview and was absolutely reduced to tears, as I am sure everyone else that watched it was too. It was heartbreaking to watch.

This fella has given so much to rugby league and to be fair, he has broken Cas's hearts on more occasions, but you know what, that just doesn't count anymore.

But, what does, is that he stays positive, and judging by the huge amount of money raised, he is well and truly loved by all in the Rugby League Family.

The nails are on for my nephew's wedding!! Eeeekkk!! I am so excited!! And, my nails match my outfit perfectly! Burgundy and one gold!! Perfection…

Well, that is me done for Christmas!!

Honestly, the roads just get mental up to Christmas, I need a rest just from the sheer stress and road rage in one day!!

I just cannot be bothered with it all!! I mean, let's face it, the shops are shut for Christmas Day only, that is one, yes one day!! That's all…

It's Wedding Day!!

I am so excited!! I cannot wait to get dressed up and get my gorgeous dress on! I have washed and dried my hair, all ready for Jase to curl it for me.. if it fucks up, I have enough time to sort it out!! Haha!!

Well, he is like a pro! Go on Jase lad! I am impressed! My hair looks bloody fantastic!! The make up, and the dress are on! I am ready...

I look absolutely, bloody, lovely, and so does my husband and son! I tell you what? We have scrubbed up well between us! I love a Christmas wedding!

We arrive at the venue, and there is a big, massive Christmas Tree in the foyer that is right in the middle of the grand hotel. It's amazing! I am like, 'wow!! Look at that tree!' Jase said, "and before you ask, no, we are not having a selfie there" alright, cocky boots, I'm only pissed off with him because that's exactly what I was going to say to him!! Anyway, we have a selfie... haha!!

We have an absolutely, amazing day at the wedding, it was lovely. I love a good wedding!

At the night party, a few of my ex-pupils were there, all wanting selfies and I posted it on social media then others were like, 'thought I was your favourite Karen?' haha!

Well, now the lovely day is over, and I am feeling happy and content, it's now one of the hardest times of the year, visiting the grave of my parents at Christmastime...

I cannot possibly visit it on Christmas Day because it absolutely breaks my heart, my whole body feels so absolutely overwhelmed, I am always distraught.

I put fresh flowers on, and a wreath, chatting away about what we've done, telling them about Brad and Sophie's wedding and then I stand back and all of a sudden, I cannot see anything because tears have rushed to my eyes and are now streaming down my face.

The overwhelming grief that I feel just gets me every year, and I cannot help it, but, once I have been, I can then start to enjoy Christmas, because after all, no matter how hard it is, life does go on...

We have been married 8 years today! I can honestly say, I am still very happy, and still very much in love with my husband, aww....

We go to one of our local restaurants for an anniversary breakfast treat before we make the trip to Aysgarth Falls for the night.

Aysgarth Falls Hotel are one of Cas Tigers sponsors and loads of people have been, so I thought, why not?

We check in at the hotel and then head down to the falls, what a beautiful place it is, full of such natural beauty, it's truly amazing.

We have THE most gorgeous anniversary meal and a few glasses of wine, it's lovely, so special, and it's just for us.

The next day, we have breakfast and then head to Stockheld Park on our way home. I've seen loads of posts on social media about it, and it always looks amazing, so Christmassy and wintery, and I want to go!

Considering it has been quite wet recently, the field where you park is so muddy it is unreal!! And all my husband is bothered about, is his mucky, muddy alloys! ffs!! It will wash....

The first place we visit is the Ice Skating Rink!! I love ice skating, even though I'm absolutely shite and daren't let go of Jase's hand, I still think I'm swanning about like Jayne Torvill!! I don't fall, yes!! Well Done Kazza!!

It's Christmas Eve, and as we have just got back from a lovely night away, we always stay in on this night, and just have a lovely chill out, ready for the big day, you can guarantee there's a few silly snapchat filters on the go and just a general fun time!

This is one of my favourite social media quotes:

'May you never be too grown up to search the skies on Christmas Eve'

Never ever for me, it's a magical, sad, happy, highly emotional time of year and I absolutely love it!!

Christmas Day!!

We get up all excited and I place my 25 years old son's 20 thousand Christmas presents on the chair, even though every year I say he's not getting a lot this year!! Haha!! And wait for him to get up!

I am dying to go in his room and say, "please get up Sam" but if I did, he would go mad! It was absolutely loads better, when he was younger, and he was so excited, and know he's like, "mam, just shut up" ha ha!

I can't wait for him to have kids, I will be one of them Granny's that just does what I want and then say, "don't tell yer Dad!" ha ha!!

I have a big, massive, fuck off present to open from Jase that I have been dying to open, but, I have contained myself! Not any longer!! What is this???? I am so excited!!

I rip the paper off, and I see a knife... I'm still smiling, but all the time, I'm thinking what actually is this?

Well, I'll tell you what this big fuck off present was shall I that I was absolutely dying to open?? It was knives, a bastard knife set!! Ffs!! As if!!

I said, "have you actually bought me some knives as a Christmas Present?"

"Well, we needed some didn't we?"

"Well, yes! But fucking hell, just buy some then, not wrap the bastard things up!"

"don't you like them?"

"Well, yes, but I was expecting something for me, and got all excited"

"Or, sorry love"

"It's okay"

Well, it's actually fucking not okay really is it? I'm gutted! I was expecting something so good!! But you know when you want to be really mad, but then you think, or bless them... at least they have bought me something! Well, that's what I thought under my anger!!

I suppose it didn't really make it any better when Sam finally got up and said, "who the fucks bought you some knives?" I said, "Jase" he said, "or, they're alright them aren't they!?" "get lost Sam!" haha!!

We always have my sister and nephew round for Christmas Day Dinner, and it is always a laugh, Sam winding my nephew up, him getting monk on, my sister going mad, ooh, it is all good fun, and making memories!

Jason's mam was working in the pub, but joined us later, after Dinner. We played online monopoly, omg! My nephew getting monk on because he wasn't winning, Sam winding my nephew up, and my mother-in-law not having a clue what she's supposed to be doing!

Laughing and swearing, drinks flowing, it's all good!! What a laugh... haha!!

So, Brad and Sophie could not make Christmas Day Dinner has planned, due to his Grandmas terminal illness, and obviously they all wanted to be together for, what quite possibly could be her last Christmas.

Instead, we have a Sunday Christmas Dinner to make up for it and omg! What a laugh that was too!!

Sam and Keane are Manchester United fans and Brad Leeds United! Both teams were playing, and honestly you would have thought we was at the game, the noise was bloody stupid!!

Whenever there was a score, regardless of the team, one of them would be cheering and shouting and then they were jumping on each other and pretend fighting, omg! It was mental, but so, so good! Such good fun and lovely to see them all having a good time!!

I love them all so much.

Happy New Year!!!

It's my 50th Birthday Year!!

I cannot wait!!

This year is going to be THE best ever.... I have a Caribbean Cruise booked the day after my actual birthday, Jamaica in May, Toronto for the Cas Game in June, Venice in September, Iceland in December and then a cruise for the new year to Dubai and Abu Dhabi to end an amazing 50th Birthday Year!!

We go into Leeds for the afternoon, and we have a really good time, a few cocktails, go for a meal in Gino's and then head home, happy days!

I always take my tree down on New Year's Day then it's done, all sorted, and, ready for when we go back to work! I absolutely love, love, love, putting the tree up, but taking it down absolutely stresses me out!!

I have elderly neighbours over the road for me and the lady has dementia and is getting quite bad, bless her, it is so sad. Her husband came over, and said to me, "Karen, if you ever see anything that doesn't look right at our house, will you just come over because if anything happens to me, I'm not sure Margaret will know what to do!" bless him!

This must have been playing on his mind, it's so sad! He then said, "you know if you notice the blinds aren't open after 9am or something" omg! I was nearly crying bless him! I said, "of course I will, don't worry, I will make sure you are okay."

This must be so sad to feel like this, he must have been thinking about it, and I just feel so sorry for them.

Before Christmas we took Alfie for his yearly check up, and the vet said that one of his testicles was bigger than the other and we should consider him been neutered.

We had noticed it had got a bit bigger, and that he had been licking it more than usual, but didn't really think anything of it, anyway, we decided that we should have him neutered, just in case something was wrong, and it spread, we would never forgive ourselves.

I am absolutely crying my eyes out when I dropped Alfie off at the vets, I said to him, "mummy loves you so much Alfie, I won't be long until I pick you back up precious baby."

I just sat in the car and cried my eyes out, roll on 5pm when I can pick him back up!

The vet's ring and I can pick Alfie up! All has gone well, and they don't think it's anything serious, but the testicles will need to be sent off to be tested just in case.

Aww! His little face is so sad! I love this dog more than anything, he's my little baby! He hasn't got a cone around his head, as they proper stress him out, so we opt for the body suit instead, it's just like a little baby romper suit with a hole out for the tail! It's so much better.

I bring him home, and we had loads of cuddles, but he just can't get comfy, he looks so sad! I lay on the rug in front of the fire with him and just lay there so he knows I am next to him!

Sam came in and said, "or Alfie mate! What have they done to you? What's naughty mummy done to you?" I said, "shut up Sam!" he said, "Mam he looks really sad!" I said, "I know he does, he will be okay though" he said, "well let's face it mam, you have just chopped his balls off" ffs Sam!! Not me personally!! Haha!!

Saw this earlier and thought, mmm....

"They say 40 is the new 30 and 50 is the new 40,

But all I know is the older I get, the more 9pm,

is the new midnight"

That is so, so true!!!

Aww! Today was Legends Day at Headingley.

All these absolute superstars from back in the day turning out for 1 last game!

Honestly, I could not really tell you what happened, because I cried all the way through!!

But, what I do know, is that when the Legend that is, took just one last run out on that field, that there wasn't a dry eye anywhere!!

What a guy!

He ran on the field to a humongous sound of chants, cheers and clapping.

His speech at the end of the game was heart wrenching.

Motor Neurone.

A terrible, cruel disease...

Omfg!! She passed!!!

How many chuffing times did she piss about changing her test times! Ffs! I was done in!! ha ha!!

Text after text after text! "Karen, can you do this date?"

"yes love"

"or hang on, there's one the day before"

"yeh, okay love, that's okay too"

Next day, "Karen, there's another test on, can you do this?"

"ffs Jess! It's just 2 hours earlier than the one you have booked!"

"yeh I know, but I think I will pass at this time and not the other!"

"Okay love"

Jeez…..

But, a pass is a pass!! And I am well chuffed for her!!

My same day birthday guy passed today too!! Yyyaaayyy!!

Honestly, all he has done every week is count down to his 18th, which has obviously reminded me how close it is to me been 50! As if!

I can still remember been 18, and that doesn't seem that long ago! Time just passes by….

Sometimes I wish I could find it in my heart to delete my social media accounts, but I absolutely 100% cannot!!

I mean, come on, how would you even know what was happening in the world if you didn't have it? And, you all know, if it's on social media, then it's got to be true! Haha!!

Anyway, my friend has been going on about the Hair Wrap, and I'm like, please no one comment on how good it is because, I will want to buy it, and no doubt, have a massive debate with myself about the justification of the bastard price!!

The comments are fab!! Ffs!! One of friends commented saying that, 'it was the best thing she has bought' another said, 'took this on the cruise with me, my hair was fab! I didn't even need to visit the hairdresser on board the ship at 'dress up' night as my wrap did it all for me'

Nnoooooo....

10 minutes later, I have email confirmation of my purchase of the Hair Wrap and a delivery date!! Ffs!!

Well, its okay, its on the monthly!! So, that's okay isn't it??

What are men like? Well, it's okay don't even think about it never mind answer it!!

Jase was talking about going on holiday and said he wanted to go to Ibiza to Café Mambos, so I said, "okay love I will have a look" then he carries on, "well, let's face it, it's always where you want to go on holiday I never get a choice" "what? Chuff me, more like you say you'll go anywhere, you're not bothered" "well, I want to go to Café Mambos for my birthday" "chill out Jase love, all you've got to do is say..." ffs!!

Have you seen the prices of fucking Ibiza!! Ffs!! Go to Caribbean for that price!! But, best not say anything, and all that... Ibiza is booked!

Then just to top it all, apparently, it's pricey as fuck when you're there too!!!

Another little quotey poos for you, which I pissed myself at!!

"Apparently, 'enough so that I don't have to hold my belly up to shave my foo foo' isn't an appropriate unit of measurement, when Lisa from the Slimming Club, asks how much weight I want to lose"

Ffs!! We all know what she means though...

Haha!!

Chapter Sixteen

The Hair Wrap is here, and here I am, Hairdresser of the Year!! Go on lass!!

All I can say, is, practice will make perfect, wont it?? Haha!

Here's another quote from Social Media...

Remember back in school in cookery class, when the teacher would ask you to bring in ingredients for the following day and your mum would say, "Tell her to fuck off! If she wants you to make a cake, she can fucking pay for it"

To be fair, its costs about 10 times as much to bake the fucker than it does to just buy one!!

The Birthday and Holiday nails are on!!! I have just gone a bit subtle, after all I am nearly 50!! Bloody 50!! Oh, my days!!

It is Brexit Day!!

Has anything changed today?

Erm, no!!

Only time will tell if this has been the correct decision...

Party Day!!

I pick my cake up from the local cake makers, and oh my! It is, THE best!! I chose a miniature schnauzer design just like my little Alfie bobs, it is amazing!! The lady that makes them, is very, very, talented!!

I park my car just round the corner from the shop and to protect the cake he clips a cardboard cake box over it.

I'm thinking ffs Karen! Do NOT drop this cake!!

It turns out, that I don't need to worry about dropping the chuffing thing, as a gust of wind comes, flips the lid up, and I cannot see Jack Shit!! Ffs!!

Anyway, all is good, its safely sat in the car!! Phew...

I am so excited for my Birthday Party!!!

I decided that instead of a full on blown buffet and party, come disco, that at my age maybe a more reserved sitdown meal, with a bit of music might be more appropriate... you know been 50 and all that! Haha!!

The venue looked amazing, I was so happy, everyone turned up that said they were coming, and a good night, was had by all...

You know when you invite ALL the family, and you know full well that they won't come, you know because of stocktakes at work and shit... ffs!

And, then them that will let you know, fucking hell just say you're not coming love!! I'm only inviting you to be kind anyway, I knew all along you wouldn't come!

But in my eyes, you were invited, you declined...

The next morning it's the local, high end restaurant for Breakfast, like you do after you've been out the night before! Yum Yum!!

I'm one of them people that always puts a thought into buying a card for any occasion and I can honestly say that some of the cards I received were pretty amazing!!

I have a pass today... I am so happy for her, it's her second attempt, and I must admit, she should have passed 1st time, it was just one of them things!!

Just for Fun...

How to Parallel Park..
1. *Pull up just passed the space*
2. *Look at how much space there is*
3. *Think Fuck That!!*
4. *Drive off....*

Hahahahahahaha!!!!

Omfg!! How poorly are we?? 2 days before we are due to go on holiday and we are ill… my throat is absolutely killing me, I feel like the back of my throat has been attacked, I'm so ill, and Jase and Sam are full of cold, coughing, and generally feeling shite, wtf is wrong with us all…

And then just to make things even worse, Storm fucking Ciara is on its way across the Atlantic!! Ffs!! We will be flying straight into it!! Great!!

It is the night before my Birthday, and, I actually feel like total and utter shite… I thought do you know what? I'm going to have an early night in the last night of my forties.. I went into the bathroom to brush my teeth and omg, I have never, ever, in my entire life felt pain in my ear like this!! Ffs!! Aaarrgggghhhhh…..

I was screaming out in pain and Jase and Sam came running into the bathroom and Sam said, "mam, are you okay?" I said, "no, no, I'm not, it's killing" when the pain finally stopped, I touched my ear, and it was bleeding.. I absolutely shit myself, am I going to die? Wtf!! I'm flying to St.Lucia tomorrow!!

Anyway, you need to always google your symptoms don't you, just to make sure you're not going to die!! Haha!!

A perforated eardrum?? You need to seek medical advise?? Ffs!!

111 it is then... she said 'I would be okay, and to just ring my GP tomorrow'.

Well, how do you think I slept?? Yep, with my poorly ear onto the pillow, just so the blood would flow out of my ear, and not flow back into my head, and then I would die!! Ffs!! Haha!!

I rang my GP, and he wants to see me...

I need to get myself to Gatwick love, not mess about with appointments.. well, I don't really mean that do I? Because let's face it, deep down I'm shitting myself!! And... if I CAN go on holiday, what if I'm ill on the plane?? Or ffs!! Let's google it!! Hahaha!!

Apparently, it is okay to fly with a perforated eardrum, its only if you've had an ear operation that you can't fly...

So, cases already packed, and off I trot to the doctors, with my "Fabulous at 50" T-Shirt, like you do...

He said, it seems I have a perforated eardrum and it's still quite congested, so he will see me again on Monday! I said, "oh, this is the problem, I'm due to fly to St.Lucia tomorrow, can I? it is my 50Th today…" he looked at his screen and said, "ooh, so it is! Happy Birthday" I said, "thankyou" whilst the doctor is staring at his computer screen….

"Erm….. I think I'll just give the ENT consultant a call at the hospital, just to make sure.."

I'm sat there just thinking ffs!! All this money I've spent, all the hard work, and for what??

Anyway, turns out I CAN fly with a perforated eardrum, but the only thing is, is that I will NOT be insured if anything happens with my ear, as it is now classed as a 'pre-existing medical condition' well, I'm just going to have to take the risk aren't I?

He wished me a Happy Birthday, and to have a good holiday!!

So, we finally set off…. Oioi!! I am SO excited, but we both still feel like absolute shite, but maybe we will be okay tomorrow…

We stop off on the way down to Gatwick for the toilet and my husband treats me to a Maccys, aww, Happy 50th love, here's a Big Mac!! Hahaha!! #makingmemories and all that!!

Check us out in The Hilton Gatwick... beautiful room and hotel, and, I'm worried sick about my ear, and about flying with it, and Jase is popping paracetamol's so room service it is!!

So, here we are on my 50th laid on the bed eating cheese sandwiches, a bag of crisps and a couple of bottles of beer! It has certainly been different!

Omg!! We are all checked in!! I actually cannot wait to get there, and, hopefully my ear will be okay...

We are about to board the plane and I feel like my heart is going to burst out of my chest!! I am so worried about my ear, or ffs, it's too late now we are on the plane, and we're off, next stop St.Lucia....

The ear has survived the flight! Yyyyaaaayyyy....

Here we are, I am actually beyond excited!! We get off the plane and straight onto a bus, ffs what about a toilet?? Bleeding hell, I always need a wee ,even when I don't need a wee!! Good job I had one before we started our descent and not wait!! Jeez.... Hahaha!!

We have a toilet stop!! Thank the lord!! Oh, hang on, we have a ticket you know like the ones you used to get in the old cinema, the ones on a roll... anyway, there better not be a queue!!

As we are walking towards the little building, there IS a queue at one side, but not the other side, ffs! Here we go, queuing for chuffing toilet... well, well, well, it's the men that are queuing, and the women are straight in!! Has that ever been known? Oi oi, I'm straight in, see ya Jase... hahaha!

We have a few selfies, like you do!! But I just want to get on the ship and get settled...

We arrive at the ship and wow, wow, wow!! it is huge!!

I am beyond excited...

After we have finally found our room, ffs, it like the fucking crystal maze... oh, and then had our safety meeting, and the Muster Stations, we can finally have a look around the ship...

We decided that we would go up to The Crow's Nest when we set sail, what an experience as we sail away out of St.Lucia, all ready for a lovely sea day the next day..

So, here we are, our first full day on our tour around paradise. We weren't sure where to eat, or what to do, so we just went to the main restaurant, Jeez, how posh is this?

I just want some toast, or something, I'm starving, but oh no, we have to order, sit there and wait, and make small talk with all these snotty fuckers, ffs! Nightmare...

When we came out, I said to Jase, "please don't tell me we have to endure this for a fucking week? Surely there must be somewhere else to eat?" Jase said, "Kaz, there must be, we will find somewhere!" I hope so...

We go to the buffet restaurant for our lunch which is much better, and we can sit where we want, thank god!!

We have a walk around the ship, and go sit on the top deck as we are sailing the Caribbean Sea, it's amazing, I feel so lucky...

We arrive back at our room and waiting for us a bottle of champagne and chocolate strawberries from Jason's brother and his wife, oh my, they are absolutely devine!

I hope I aren't pissed drinking this champers before I go for something to eat, let all them snotties start, and I'll be straight in! Johnnie 10 men when I'm pissed! Haha!!

So, as we are waiting in the queue in the restaurant, I said to Jase, "get a table for 2, I can't be arsed with conversation I'm knackered!!" he said, "I know, neither can I"

Thank goodness, we've got a table for 2!!

We sit down on a table for 2, with a table for 2 at either side of us, we order drinks and then it starts..

"have you had a good day? Are you looking forward to tomorrow? Do you have any trips booked..." well, you can't be ignorant can you? So, we have to answer.... Chat, chat, fucking chat!!

Now, we're on a table for fucking 2, that you have to wait for, now don't you think that that means I don't want chit chat, and to make small talk?? Fuck me! Shut up talking to us!!

Tonight is 'dressing up' night! I am so excited we have matching gold outfits! Oh hi, check me and r Jase out!! Haha!!

We get ready, and to be fair, we both look amazing... I have a long gold sequined cowl neck dress, with a side split on the leg, and Jase has a light gold suit, we actually do look the dogs bollocks, and I can't wait to have some professional photographs took...

Everyone is looking at us, we are definitely turning heads!!

This is sssoooo not us!!

But, you know what, we actually enjoyed it!! And, just for the record the photos were amazing too....

St.Marteen... I have one VERY excited husband!! To be fair, I'm pretty excited myself!!

We are going on an organised boat trip which moors up just off Mayo Beach, and we are in prime place to see the planes come into land, very low, above the beach.

It is a fab trip, the captain of our boat has the frequency channel on for the planes, so he knows when one is on finals into the airport, its fab, Jase is so happy to have seen this, it is amazing!!

Well, now there is thick, and then there is thick... a plane is about to take off and there are people purposely stood at the fence waiting to get blown away from the plane taking off!!

Fuck that!! Dickheads!! I'll just sit here videoing you all for a laugh on Social Media later!!

What a day!! It's been fab!! We sail back to The Ship, still buzzing from an amazing day at Mayo Beach.

Time to get ready for this evening, and, fuck it! If they start tonight, I'm telling them about my hubby been a pilot!! Well, I know it's on a PPL, but they haven't got one of them have they!!

Well, they started, didn't they?? Oh, so, where's everyone been today then? Mayo Beach I guess?? Fuck off knobhead, I suppose you've been 6 million times before on your previous cruises… ffs!!!

Anyway, fuck em, here goes… in my poshest voice, haha! "oh yes, we have! It was amazing! Jason has his PPL so he IS a PILOT and CAN fly planes so today was amazing for us.." "oh really" looking down their posh noses at us!! "that's amazing" well, it would have been more believable that you were happy about it, if you'd have straightened your sour faces!! Haha!!

And all this time Jase is giving me that 'please don't start' look..

Come on Captain Jase, it is time for cocktails….

Today we are in Antigua! Oh my, what a beautiful place…

We have a Rib Boat trip booked, god only knows how this is going to go, I mean, let's face it, I'm no Barbie, and this is a small boat...

Well, all I can say is that my husband thinks he's fucking James Bond ripping across the Caribbean Sea, and I'm bouncing up and down like a big fat round ball, and then to top it all the bastard safety catch which is tied around my waist comes off the back of the boat, and the engine cuts out! Great!! Just Great!!

The guy comes back to us, clips it back in and off we go again.. I said to Jase, "how fucking embarrassing, this is your fault, you're going too fast over them big waves, it's a wonder I haven't broke my back, you're a dickhead!"

We stop at a coral reef, and it's amazing, personally I didn't go in the sea because I'd have shit myself trying to get back into the little rubber boat!!

AND... I'm driving it going back, he can bounce all over this time, I'm having something to hold onto, none of this just holding onto his waist shite!!

All I can say is, what an experience that was!! I did enjoy it really!!

It's another Sea Day today, and when we went into the bar at night the band was playing, 'hey, we're going to

Barbados' I am so excited, I have always wanted to go to Barbados, it looks lovely...

Well, it was a bit rocky last night on the ship! Jase was shitting himself! Haha! He's like, "Kaz, it's not safe this" and going onto the balcony, but all the time I'm singing to him, "hey! We're going to Barbados!!"

It's Valentine's Day, and we are in Barbados.. what better place could you wish to be...

We decide on a beach day.

We get off the ship, and see what's happening with transport, as we are absolutely clueless as to what we are supposed to do!! This guy asks us where we want to go, and points us in the direction of this taxi, well, what a laugh this turned out to be!!

The women driving our taxi was absolutely crazy, and this American man needed a barber's to have his haircut!! Wtf!! Anyway, she has us all singing away on the journey to the beach, drops this American fella off at the barber's and we're all good...

We get a couple of sunbeds and a brolly for my little ginner hubby, and an ice bucket full of bottles of beer.. ahh, this is the life, on a beach in Barbados on

Valentine's Day with my husband, drinking beer, and just watching the world go by... absolute bliss... we have a lovely time, and then head back to the ship as we have an Evening Sunset boat trip booked...

We board the catamaran for our Sunset Trip, it's a bit cloudy, and no sun, but hey ho, who cares? We are in Barbados and I'm so happy!!

Jase decides he's going to talk to the captain of the boat?? Wtf?? Anyway, he leaves me sat downstairs looking out to sea, when next thing, one of the guides is sat next to me wanting a selfie! Haha!! Go on lad!!

It seems the weather back home has been quite bad, with Storm Ciara and then Storm Dennis looming, there are some concerns about the flights, but I'm sure we will be okay...

It's time to head back home... we have really enjoyed it, but there is a lot on the cruise that are totally up their own arses, and that's just not us!!

We have breakfast, then head off the ship for one last look around Barbados.

We see one of our neighbours, who is also an old school friend, and she is on the ship for her 50th too, but she just got here last night, and we are leaving today.

We have a few drinks and then head over to the departure rooms on the ship, but all is not as it seems…

Storm Dennis is causing absolute havoc back home and some of the flights have been delayed! Fortunately, ours is not one of them so we get on the bus, and head over to Grantley Adams Airport for the flight back to Gatwick.

Pleasant flight until we get near home, and it's a bit rocky, but we have no concerns, we have faith in the pilot to land us safely back at Gatwick, after all he will have had training for landing in bad weather, won't he??

We start our descend into Gatwick, and honestly, it's pretty bad going to be fair, next thing we have an aborted landing, and the cabin crew are quick to reassure everyone that this is common, and we have nothing to worry about.

We look at the screen in front of us and the flight line is straight up the middle of the country to Manchester!! We just look at each other and say, "they better be fucking joking! We best not be landing at Manchester!!"

Oh no! it's no joke! We have an aborted landing at Gatwick, and he is going to try and land at Manchester!! Ffs!! Our car is at Gatwick and Manchester is a hour from home...

So, we land at Manchester, and the air stewardess said, "we have just landed here temporary, and we will just wait half hour because there was a lot of air traffic around Gatwick, so that's why we're here and we will attempt to land back at Gatwick shortly.

Captain Jase gets his Flight Radar 24 up to see what's happening, and there is a lot of air traffic around Gatwick, and a lot of holding patterns going on, but planes are landing.

Next thing we are all departing the plane, we need to get our suitcases and buses will be put on for us to get back to Gatwick!! Ffs!! You are actually joking!!

We all get on the buses ready for our bleeding bus trip back to Gatwick, the most annoying thing is, is that 1 hour into our bus journey, the plane landed back at Gatwick!! Ffs!! That pissed me off even more!!

We get off the bus, it's absolutely pissing it down, we have to get the bus to pick the car up, the car parking receptionists are tearing their hair out, it's a massive walk to the car as the parking lots at the front are full of cars that the owners haven't been able to pick up, but I'm just glad to be on our way home in our own car..

We stop at the services on the way back home, it's raining, it's freezing, we're tired, and it seems an absolute lifetime since we were in Barbados not only yesterday!!

Absolutely devastating news that a lovely television presenter has taken her own life, it is so, so, sad...

You always hope and pray that none of your family would ever feel so low that they feel the need to take their own life, it is okay to feel sad, it is okay to feel troubled, it is okay not to be okay, but you know what? There is always people there for you, and don't ever forget that..

"In a world where you can be anything, be kind"

Chapter Seventeen

Back to work it is!! Let's see what the joys of driving around I have missed! I am sure it will feel like I've never been away!!

I have a first time pass today!! Love, love, love first time passes!! I must admit, she had been driving with her Mum and Dad, and was pretty confident, so there was no reason why she shouldn't have passed first time.

I am all for private practice with the parents, why not? It seems to make them more confident and they are used to driving in a car without any dual controls, but the main thing for me is that the parents can proper bollock them if they do stupid stuff, where as I, have to, 'remain professional' at all times!! Haha!!

Well, its nice to see all these statuses about been kind, and how it makes others feel, which is good, I'm all for that, but what does really piss me off is the same people that are making out that they are Mother Theresa are the same ones that see a post and share it no matter what with no feelings or regard for anyone else!!

Ooh Look!!! Have you seen this!! I'm sharing it!! Erm... why?? Do you even know if it's true? Do you even know the person? Why are you seeing the bad in it? Is it genuine? You just don't know do you? If it's nothing to do with you, then don't share it!!

'In a world where you can be anything, be kind'

Just a real funny thing about people sharing stuff though... I once remember seeing a post someone had shared and it was about this woman who had gone missing 3 years previous, and one of my friends, who is 80 years old, commented on it and said, "bloody hell Pete! Be hopes they have found her, its bloody 3 years ago! It's a long time to be missing!!" ffs!! Hahaha!!

Or, when people share stuff about a missing dog in Texas or something!! Well, it's not going to be over here in England is it now!! Don't people even look at what they are sharing!!! It's crazy!!

Another first time pass today!! Woo woo!! Go Kazza!! I am so pleased he passed, he's such a lovely lad, well done mate!!

And I have a pass today too.. now this girl, this is life at it's hardest... she wasn't very confident anyway, and she finally passed her theory after telling me how she wouldn't be able to pass it and blah, blah, blah, just get it booked love!! Hahaha!!

So, we have the theory passed and we are planning on booking the driving test for the August Holidays, but then the absolute worst thing happens.. her mum, an old school friend of mine, dies suddenly aged 48! Omg! I am devastated for her...

She continued with her lessons, just for a bit of normality really, and someone to talk to, someone to understand her.

Even though we are Driving Instructors, the things you talk about and the things people share with you, it's like a counselling session, but you know what? If it helps someone to talk on their driving lessons, and put a massive trust in you, and they feel better for talking about whatever is troubling them, then, I'm happy with that.

So back to my lovely pupil who's just passed her driving test.. it's took us absolutely ages to get to a point where she feels confident enough to take her test, It's been a tough few months, and we've had tears and laughter, but most off all, she knows I'm always there for her.

Not only is she still grieving, but her nanna has dementia and her grandad COPD so she is now caring for both of them too..

I am absolutely over the moon that she has passed her Driving Test!!

If anyone deserves some good news, then it's her!! Well Done my lovely!!

I have another pass today!! Now, this lovely has no confidence whatsoever, we've had loads of lessons and on her first attempt she just couldn't complete the test and the examiner had to abandon it because she just couldn't carry on..

We have the test rebooked as her theory is about to run out... when I pick her up, she gets into the car crying..

"hey, come on, you can do this!"

"Karen, I actually can't"

"Do you drive your own car? Does your fella think you're a good driver? Do I say you're a good driver?"

"well, yeah, but I'm not!!"

"yes, you are! Come on sweetie, we can do this.."

10 minutes later, we set off for her Driving Test.

We have a good drive before, which pleases me, but once they get in the car with the examiner it's a different story.

I'm worried sick whilst she's out on her test, because she is a fab driver, just needs to get over her nerves, and lack of confidence.

She arrives back at the test centre, and I'm looking into the car, and next thing, she bursts into tears and looks at me, and can't believe she's actually passed her driving test!!

You can do it! Just believe in yourself!

I have persuaded Jase to sponsor Castleford Tigers Women's team! We are having the flight simulator name on the shorts, and tonight is the Shirt Presentation Night.

I am so excited! I love the women's game!!

Happy 11th Birthday to our little precious Alfie!! He might only be a dog to some, but to us, he is our little baby! As if it has been nearly 11 years since we picked up our little bundle of joy! He is the Best!!

It has just been on the news that because of this flu virus from china, we need to keep our distance from others! How can I do that in my job? I am sat next to a different person every hour!

Surely, it can't be that bad...

I am not really sure if I should be working or not? I can't social distance like they've been saying on the news, so what am I supposed to do?? I mean, there's queues all over, and it seems people are stocking up on food and that, and panic buying freezers and shit! Ffs! What is happening...

People seem to be looking at me strangely today as I'm driving around on my lessons... should I be working? I just don't know..

It's been on the news again about social distancing, and this flu virus, and I'm confused!

I tell Jase about all the queues at the shops and stuff, and we have a deep conversation, about whether we should actually be working, and what about earning money? What will we do?

We decide we should stay home, and to close our businesses, but, have we made the right decision?

I really don't know! It's all a bit up in the air at the minute...

So, my food delivery arrives, and he says, "sorry love, no toilet roll, everyone's gone mad for it! It's Smartprice, is that okay?" "IT'S SMARTPRICE???? You are joking mate, aren't you? That's fingers going through" haha!! He said, "I'd keep it if I was you there's none left on shelves!!" ffs! What is happening??

Boris Johnson addresses the nation, and we MUST stay home! What?? What is happening?? How actually bad is this virus?? Bloody hell, I really do not know what to think!! This is going to bad...

"Maybe Mother Nature wants her Earth back, for just a little while, she wants some time for the land to heal, for the people to heal, for the treadmill to stop, and let everything and everyone breathe, we have all been so worried about our beautiful planet, searching for answers, trying to play our part, making small changes, and hoping it was enough, so maybe Mother Nature stepped in herself. Stories are appearing all over the world, of nature thriving, skies clearing, Dolphins swimming in Venetian Canals, Ducks in Roman Fountains, Wild Boars with her babies in the streets of Italy. Maybe, Mother Nature wants her Earth back, For just a little while, And maybe, she is telling us to protect the weak whilst this rebirth takes place. So maybe, we should do what Mother Nature says, She's been waiting a long time for us to change. AND we DIDN'T.."

Driving Tests are suspended for 3 months! 3 Months?? Bloody hell, okay then... so, I am not working for the next 3 months?? Wow!! I do not know what to think of all this!! It has never been known...

It seems that the government are going to pay 80% of people's wages!! I cannot believe this!! Wow!! The GOVERNMENT are paying people's wages? Chuffing hell, now this is serious, I am getting quite worried here...

It seems an absolute lifetime, before Rishi Sunak makes a decision on the pay for the Self Employed! It's 80% average over the last 3 years, I'm happy with that!! It is quite a relief that we are going to get paid, but it's still pretty scary the amount of money that the government are paying out!! This virus must be pretty bad...

We have elderly neighbours and they are all pretty worried about going out, and catching what seems to be a highly contagious virus that you cannot see.. we don our shopping lists, keeping our distance, queue at every single shop that we go to, but the main thing is, that we are keeping our elderly neighbours safe.

Just on the shopping theme, wtf is it with bleeding newspapers and old people? Ffs!! 'And a paper please', 'ooh, you couldn't get us a paper, could you?' 'Ooh, a paper please, don't forget it's Saturday so make sure the TV Mag is in otherwise we won't know what's on the tv!!' Are you fucking kidding me?? Ffs!! Haha!!

We now know that this is called Coronavirus, and that we will be having a daily update on the virus and anything associated with it and what we need to do!

We must 'stay home, save lives and protect the NHS'

Well then, 3 months then! Okay then, erm, well, what we going to do? I have never had any time off with pay! I look around my house, and I decide I might as well get the paint out!! Well, what else are we going to do for the next 3 months??

You know what Jase? I'm going to do 10 thousand steps a day, lose weight, get fit, oh hi! I'm on it!!

We go for some lovely walks down by the river, its lovely to get some fresh air, and you know what? Life's pretty good, the weathers good, and, to be quite honest I'm pretty happy with been off!! I am certainly going to make the most of this....

It seems everyone and their Granny is painting their fences!! And it seems all a kind of slate grey colour... oh, that'll be us too!! Haha!! Well, at least we are all matching!! And let's face it, the weathers been pretty decent too, which makes a change!!

Ah Fuck it! Can't be arsed with this walking malarkey every day, and it's a bit too hot! I will just sit in garden and sunbathe instead!! Well, until 5pm, when I have to be inside for the Coronavirus Update!!

Jase decides he is going to order a couple of model planes and build them from scratch, paint them, bang a motor in them, and then fly them on the field at the back of us!! Ffs!! This is all I need when I am trying to sunbathe, a fucking silly little plane spoiling the silence!! Haha!!

Someone suggested that at 8pm every Thursday, we should stand on our doorsteps, and clap for carers. Little did we know that this would become a Thursday night ritual, and we would even have Boris stood outside No.10 clapping to show his appreciation for our wonderful NHS.

Oh no!! Elemis is Today's Special Value on the shopping channel!! Well, I don't know what to do! I haven't got any money, and I can't apply for this SEISS grant until next month! But, its Elemis… Fuck it! I don't care how skint I am, I still have to look good and young and omg! I can't let my face get all wrinkly and old whilst we're in lockdown!! Haha!!

Hang on! What's crack here with all these deliveries like?? Another fucking model plane and I'm thinking twice about buying Elemis!! Well, I tell you what, he can pay for it, if we've got money to waste on toys!! Haha!!

Well, our elderly neighbours are absolutely loving the fact that we are off work!! The weathers great, which I suppose makes been locked down a bit easier, at least people can get out for a bit of exercise and fresh air, and not stuck in the house all the time!

Anyway, our neighbours are chatting away all the time, it seems we've had a lot of catching up to do after working our arses off so long!! It's nice to just be out of the 'Rat Race' for a little time, and just take each day as it comes...

Chapter Eighteen

Jase has been shitting himself flying these little model planes on the field at the back of us, just in case the police come, and tell him off!! So, he's on the field flying them, and me and Sam are watching out of the bedroom window, next thing the plane gets stuck in the tree... ffs!!!

He runs in to get the sweeping brush to throw up into the tree, to try and knock the plane out!! Oh shit!! The brush has got stuck in the tree too!! Sam is like, "ffs! What an idiot"

One of our neighbour's lads comes out with his rugby ball, and they throw that into the tree to try and knock them out. It gets close and by this time there is a few people watching, a bit of entertainment on their daily walks!!

Ffs!!! The ball is now stuck in the tree, along with the plane, and the brush!! Could you, actually, really ,make this shit up!!

The little night in shining armour, arrives with his ladders, he's a roofer so he used to going up them! At last, the ball is out, the brush it out and the bastard plane too!! Ffs!!

Well, a bit of lockdown entertainment if nothing else, oh, and it passed a hour on...

It's, 'Clap for Carers' again tonight, and this time we have fireworks and the whole shebang!! It's so emotional, the NHS are working extremely hard along with ALL the key workers and we should be extremely grateful.

Boris Johnson is in hospital with Coronavirus! Wtf!! Omg!! This is scary shit!! Not just because our Prime Minister has caught the virus, but just in general. How on earth has all this happened? How has it escalated into this? Did it really start in China with a bat? Jeez... they will be some questions asked after all this.

Well, we have decided that we get rid of all our crap from the house and the garage, it's all a shit tip, and to be fair the garage has needing sorting for quite some time, but it has been actually finding the time to get it done!!

We order a skip, a large one at that, and we fill it within an hour!! Ffs!! A bastard hour and its full!! AND... we still have a load of shit to get rid of!! We ring the skip company to come and pick it up and leave us another empty one...

We fill the second skip, and, feel very accomplished with our day!! I'm not so sure what the big deal is with the neighbours, haven't they ever seen a fucking skip before!! Well, maybe not that full, and maybe not 2 in a day!! Haha!!

I always love it when people post funny things on social media, and today this tickled me..

'If anyone has been out on the roads recently, now you know why it only took your Dad 10 hours to pass his test!!'

This is so fucking true!! It must be one of the most annoying things ever!! 'here, mi Dad only had 10 lessons and he passed, he wants to know if I can book my test?' well, back in day, there was Jack Shit traffic on the road, not a lot of dickheads like there is now, and the test was easier!! So, in a nutshell, 'NO, YOU CAN'T!!' and if your Dad thinks you're the dogs doodah's, then get him to take you out!!

Well, it seems that Jamaica is not happening.. another 50th Birthday Year holiday that has been cancelled!! This was going to be a right year, but it has turned out it's a 'stay at home' kind of year instead!! I am sure it will be okay for next year, but I'm going to get my money back anyway!!

Fuck Me!! How actually bad is everyone's hair!! Ffs!! I've seen some right 'Covid Cuts' on social media haha!! I'm just leaving my roots to just grow, I mean let's face it, we're not going anywhere, soon are we?? In fact, come to think, my hair will probably be in much better condition without all this bleach on it!!!

Boris is out of hospital! I tell you what, he's had it a bit bad has lad!! Bloody hell, just goes to show, anyone can get it, you've got to be really careful, it's crazy!

Oioi!! What about Captain Tom?? That's 100 years old Captain Tom! What a man!!

It just goes to show with the right media coverage, miracles can happen! All that money that he has raised is absolutely fantastic! Hats off to him!!

Well Done...

I have decided that I'm going to turn my little spare bedroom into a 'Boudoir' Check me out! Fucking 'Boudoir' go on Kazza lass!!

I have big plans for this! My friend has the most amazing vintage furniture company, and I am not going to lie, I could buy everything!! It is fab!! I decide to buy a Queen Anne dressing table from her and I am trawling Ebay for the accessories... I am in heaven...

I have light grey walls, a wooden floor with a baby pink rug, dusky pink crushed velvet curtains, and a Navy Bluey Black dressing table, wow! I lurrvvv it!! My very own little Boudoir...

We have another little parcel delivery, ooh it's not a plane! What can it be?? Alloy Gators? Wtf are they like?? Ffs!! He's like a little kid!! He's got a black car with red Alloy Gators!! Jeez... apparently they look 'mint' right okay love, nice... "do you want some for your car Kaz? Save your alloys when learners curb it" nah, you're alright Jase thanks... haha!!

We're still on with the Coronavirus updates, and it is still pretty scary stuff, and pretty serious, but you know what actually pisses me off big time, is the stupid fucking questions that the media ask!! Don't they even think about what they are asking? Honestly, absolutely thick as fuck some of these dickheads!! People must just sit at home and think, 'hey up, what shite's going to come out of their mouth today!!'

I wonder if, in about 20 years time, we will be saying to our kids, "during the Coronavirus..." we will be like Albert from Only Fools!! Haha!! And our kids will be like ffs! Here we go again...

Well, I have bought some face coverings for my return to work! I am a bit scared to be fair, I mean let's face it, I haven't been at work for over 3 months!! I can still drive, so that is a plus!! I have got all my procedures in place, hand sanitiser, the lot!! And, more importantly, I have requested that ALL my pupils wear face coverings and that I will be too.

We all proper used to take the piss out of people wearing masks, didn't we? And look at us all now! Cannot leave the house without one!!

How actually slack am I? I was putting the dish back inside the slow cooker whilst it was still full, and I put my arm right over the spout on the kettle whilst it was boiling!! Ffs!! But, you know when it is one of them instances, when you know its burning you, but there's fuck all you can do about it because you would drop the food!!

My arm was straight under the cold tap!! You could actually see the shape of the spout on my arm, and where the steam had gone up it, it had concertinaed my skin!! Wtf!! It's crazy!!

It was actually killing, but, I was been a brave little soldier!

The next day, my arm didn't look too cracking, so I went to our local UTC, the Urgent Treatment Centre that was our old A&E hospital, but I did get seen to straight away, which was good, and came out with a big fuck off bandage on my arm!! Ffs!!

Note to self – don't be a dick near the steam from the kettle!!

The local flying club where Jase goes is open!! He's desperate to go up in the plane, so I agree to go with him! I'm not that bothere but, bless him, he wants me to! As long as we are from the same household, then it's okay.

We fly over our house, and take some good pictures, and all in all we have a good afternoon.

Before lockdown, we were planning on having a new bathroom, obviously this went tits up, but now we are back thinking about it, and one of our local bathroom shop, Castlewater Bathrooms in Castleford has opened back up, so we go take a look.

The guy does a plan and asks us which way we would like our towel rail? Which way we would like our towel rail?? Wtf kind of question is that? I'm confused!! So, I look at him and say, "well, there's only 1 way isn't there?" he said, "no! you can have them either way" I'm looking at him thinking, are you taking piss here mate! I thought all towel rails were vertical?? A horizontal towel rail?? Nah, mate, never heard anything as stupid in my life!! Haha!!

We came out of the shop, and Jase said, "there's no need to make a big deal out of the towel rail like that!" I said, "Jase fuck off, that's the most ridiculous thing I've heard in my life! It has actually blown my mind!" fucking hell.. wouldn't that just be a radiator then?? Ffs! I don't know! That's actually sent me over the edge!! A 'horizontal' towel rail?? Nah….

Yyaaayyyy!!! I finally have some money!!! After 3 long months I have been paid!!

I am eternally grateful for this money! I owe most of it now, but hey ho! That's life!!

It has just been announced, that before you get on a plane, you will need to have your temperature took, well, I'm not sure about that, I'm always red hot, with my menopausal outbursts!! Haha!! But, apparently, a hot flush does not affect your overall temperature! Phew! That's good to know, or I wouldn't be going anywhere!!

So, it is all about a certain politician at the minute, and debating if he broke the Coronavirus rules and all that, so it's the health secretary doing the Coronavirus update, and when it's question time, a reporter, asks him about politician, he answers the question in a very quick few words then, just cuts him off dead and goes to the next reporter!!

The news reporter is gutted!! He just throws himself back in his chair!! Actually ,funny as fuck that!! Haha!!

Just to sum up 2020 so far…

'2020 is a unique leap year, it has 29 days in February, 180 days in March, 9 months in April and so far, we are 6 years into May!'

It actually did feel like that didn't it??

I needed a sweeping brush from B&M, and I thought, I can't be arsed with all this queuing, I am going to go first thing, I will be there at 8am, straight in straight out, boom! Done!! Oh, my word, who are you kidding Kazza?? 10 to 8 and there is 18 people in front of me!! And yes, I did stand in the queue and count!! Haha!!

Anyway, I get my brush, in, out, done, home!!!

The plan for our new bathroom is finalised, with the towel rail vertical like it should be… we have decided to get rid of the bath and just have a shower, I am not really sure if this is a good idea? Not sure if I will miss actually having a bath, or if it will be the best thing we have done! Only time will tell…

Jase is on with his Social Distancing signs and getting the simulator 'Covid Safe' along with having a Risk Assessment done! I'ts all new territory is this, who would have thought all companies would have to be doing some like this, in this day and age??

We all know how extremely important our key workers have been in the last couple of months, and I am so pleased that driving tests have continued for them. And, also, to the Driving Examiners that are conducting the tests in this global pandemic.

My lovely Michaela has her driving test today! I really do hope she passes.. she has been working non-stop in a care home, making sure that all the residents are looked after, but at the same time she could potentially be putting herself and her family at risk, but these amazing carers do not think like that, there main priority is the care that they are giving..

Yyyaaayyy!! She passes!! I am so pleased!! Well Done my Lovely!!

Well, that is my one and only key worker done,and know its back home to see how long we are off work for...

I am sat watching the television, and Interflora pulls up outside, I'm looking all confused, and she gets out of the car with THE biggest bunch of gorgeous Lillies you have ever seen!! Omg!! They are from Michaela!! They are, absolutely, beautiful!!

I message her, and tell her that are, absolutely, fantastic, but, she shouldn't have done, even though I'm grateful, it's still my job. But, at the same time, it is really nice to know that, you are appreciated.

Happy 26th Birthday to my amazing son!! I love him more that life itself. Can't tag him on social media as I'm still blocked haha!! Maybe next year…

Now it is my husband's birthday!! Happy Birthday Jase!!!

Not only is it a lockdown birthday, but we are having our bathroom fitted!! Not that we could have gone anywhere anyway, but now, we definitely can't!! I did get him a Lager and Chocolate hamper, so happy days and all that!!

Omg!!! The Hairdressers are back open!!! Let me get booked in!!!! Yes!!!! I have a hair appointemt!! Get In!!!!

Should have been jetting off to Toronto for the Cas Game today, but that isn't happening is it!!

We had it all planned out with our friends!! Rugby Game, Niagra Falls, CNN Tower, well, that has just stayed as a plan...

Love my social media quotes and this is one of my absolute faves..

'Good Morning All, So, what the Fuck are we all offended by today'

I mean, let's face it! People are offended by absolutely anything these days!! Haha!!

Can you image what our elders from 40 years ago would think of today's generation!! I absolutely dread to think...

The bathroom is complete! Wow! Just wow!! Its fab!! Small, minimalistic and plain, just how I like it!! You have still got to have all the right accessories, though don't you??

I place a 'Fluffy Towels' Yankee Candle on the windowsill, very nice.. now, we all know that this is obviously NOT, under any circumstances, must this be lit!! it is purely for DECORATION purposes... haha!!

I tell you something this cancelled holiday money is coming in well handy!! We have a new carpet fitted in Sam's bedroom today, don't get me wrong, he needed one, but, again, it's been finding the time!!

This proper tickled me, because I tell you something it's so frustrating...

'now that we have everyone washing their hands correctly, next week, it's how to use indicators at roundabouts'

This refunded holiday money is going far I can tell you!!

We decide that we are just going to replace our original cupboard doors and worktops in the kitchen to keep the cost low, and then we can do that ourselves, rather than waste money getting someone in to do it.

I am just going to have a freestanding cooker and fridge freezer, because even though integrated looks amazing, it's a bastard when it breaks... I had some years ago, and it was the best thing, I loved it!! But, when one broke, I had to replace with a normal fridge and separate freezer, and I hated it! Never again!!

Aww!! We get a lovely card and present from our neighbours thanking us for looking after them in Lockdown. Bless them! To be fair it gave us something to do too, so good for us all!! But, none the less, it is nice to be appreciated in such a difficult time..

Our little break to Venice is cancelled... but, its better to be safe than sorry! The hotel looked amazing too, it was close to Rialto Bridge, and I was proper looking forward to going on a Gondola! Can you imagine! I would have been shitting myself getting in, when it's wobbling like fuck, but all making memories I suppose!!

Driving Lessons can resume!! Thank the Lord!! Oh hang on, I'm not mentally prepared to go back next week, AND, we are having a new carpet fitted in our living and dining room, (cancelled holiday money) so, I will go back the week after.. haha!! What's another week!!

Well, it's a bit of a mad rush now! Ffs!! So, I better get these kitchen floor tiles up pretty sharpish!!! I am chip, chip, chipping a fucking way at these floor tiles and I'm getting angrier by the minute!!

Lino has been stuck on top of lino, on top of stick on floor tiles, on top of the original tiles!!! I am absolutely tearing my bastard hair out!! Ffs!! Who's idea was it to even have a new kitchen?? Haha!!

My hands are ripped to shreds, and I've proper got the monk on big time!! It's an absolute nightmare, and, its stinks like you wouldn't believe!! You know that musty, old, damp, wet horrible smell that you get if you go into an old hotel where they don't have the heating on, and it hits you as soon as you walk in? well, that's how my kitchen smells, rank…

I'm just sat chilling on the sofa, and next thing Sam is stood over me, looking at my hair, and he said, "ere Mam, what actually colour is your hair? It's like blonde, brown and then bits of grey! Ffs Mam, that's bad!!" cheeky little fucker!!

Right, let's get this laminate flooring up ready for this new carpet tomorrow! I can't wait!!

Ffs!! Some of the tiles that are the original ones have blown and cracked!!

Jase is like, "Kaz, just leave them!" "just fucking leave them!! How the fuck can we do that?? We will be walking along, and it'll be crunching underneath our feet" what a Dick Head!!

Omg!! It actually takes us, what seems like a lifetime!! We are getting so pissed off, and Jase is getting angry as fuck, which I find quite funny because he is the most placid person you could wish to meet!! Haha!!

Some of the tiles just come up because they are broken, but the others are stuck down, sorry, I will rephrase that!! They are super fucking glued down, and we have to chip away, at each little fucking bit, ffs!! It is having our life!!!

Finally, we are done!!! It has been a nightmare!! Jase goes straight to shop for some beer, and sits outside, whilst I give it a quick wash over!! And I say to him, "well, it's done now love, and just think how nice it will be when the new carpet's down tomorrow". Mrs Positive and all that!!

The carpet is fitted!! Omg!! It looks fab!! It is absolutely years since I've had a carpet in the room, it's been laminate for that long, I've forgot how nice a carpet is... mmm.... It is so soft and lovely, and I love it!!!

Chapter Nineteen

Here we go again…

'How to piss off your Teenager!'
1. *Say Good Morning!*
2. *Sing any song from the 80's*
3. *Say I love you in public*
4. *Tag them on social media*
5. *Breathe*

It is hairday!!! My roots, are absolutely horrendous!! I know that, along with everyone else in the country at the minute, but I am so excited!!! My hair will be back to normal….

It is finally back to work day!!! Whatever will today bring?? Back to pissing everyone off on the roads!! Yyaayyy!! Happy Monday folks!!

Why is everyone confused with the new lockdown rules?? Ffs!! Personally, I don't think the rules are difficult!! I am sure that's not just me!! Maybe it is because I am a proper rule person anyway, so, maybe that's why I haven't found sticking to the rules so hard…

This popped up on my memories and this could not, be more true in our house!!

Some parents run a tight ship, I run a pirate ship, there is some swearing, some drinking, and a touch of mutiny from the tiny raider I created!

Hahaha!! That is fab!! We've all been there with the little shits!!

This is Jase all over, I just do not know what goes through his tiny little mind!! Ffs!! Anyway... Jase is cracking on with getting the kitchen done, and today he's fitting the new sink.

I come home from work all excited, and Jase had taken the bowl out of the old sink, and I'm not joking... he left the cups and plates in the bowl, didn't wash them up, just put the bowl on the floor in the kitchen, with the dirty crockery in it!! Ffs!! He's not right in head!! Haha!!

I was on a lesson earlier, and this stupid idiotic woman decided to overtake a parked vehicle, and was very, very close to us!! I was furious!! The silly cow! Why would you even do something like that when a learner is coming towards you?

I grabbed the wheel to steady and guide us through the tiny space. The funny thing is, I was that mad that I took my face covering off to shout at her!! Ffs!! My pupil was laughing her head off!! She said, "why have you took your mask off?" I said, "well, she needs the full effect of my angry face!!" I mean, let's face it, there's no point in just seeing the eyes is there? They need the full 'Kazza Stare' haha!!

OiOi!! Tonight, we are out out!!! Omg!! It has been a long time!! We just stay local but how nice is a bit of freedom? A bit of normality? Its fab!!

I saw this quote earlier and it proper made me chuckle....

'Ripping off your mask when you get back in the car is the new taking your bra off when you get home!'

That's ace!!!

Freshly plastered walls... how gorgeous is that smell? Mmmmm.... I can't wait until the kitchen is done! It will look amazing... that's the kitchen that we just changing the cupboard doors, the worktops, the cooker, and the fridge freezer, ended up been a complete revamp!!

Once we removed the cupboards there was a bit on the back wall that needed plastering, and when we took the top cupboards down and it looked a lot bigger, so, we decided to take the bottom cupboards out too, and make it into a bit of a kitchen diner, rather than just a kitchen!!

The kitchen is finally done and looks amazing!!

I am so happy with it!! It looks all brand new and lovely, and ooh, its fab!! It is funny how if you put your mind to it, you can really create a beautiful room by doing most of the things yourself, and of course a little imagination, or in my case all my home styling books! This is the time when Jase shits himself, because he knows I will have some ideas throwing about in my head!! Haha!!

Well, it might not have been the 50th Birthday Year I had planned, but I tell you what, I have an amazing house, and this certainly wouldn't have been the case if we could have gone on holiday!!

Its GCSE day…

How much pressure is on kids these days?? Ffs! Sometimes it horrendous!! At the end of the day, isn't your kid been happy the most important thing??

Just my opinion... Always make sure your kids happiness comes first, and not your social ego or community status...

Last night I was on social media, and this 'friend' of mine commented a bit of a sarcastic comment on my kitchen pictures, but you know when you think, 'no, she didn't mean it like that' but, then it plays on your mind, and you think, 'you know what? She DID, fucking mean that!!'

Anyway, I went back on her comment the next morning, and she had removed it!! I was mad as fuck!! So, she DID mean it like I thought she did, didn't she?? Friend my arse!! They are just jealous!! Silly bitch!! Haha!!

We are out, out again!! Making the most of this little bit of freedom we have got!! We sometimes go into our local club and I have a little game of bingo! It isn't big money, I just love playing!!

But, you know what's it's like when you're in a local working men's club, they all have their own seats, and, if you're an outsider then that's it!! Anyway, I only go and win the bingo, don't I?? ffs!! They are in uproar!! Bollocks to 'em, it pays for a kebab and the taxi home!!!

We have decided on a road trip to the coast!! Yes!! It's been ages!! We have a lovely walk along the beach, lovely fresh air, and just a total chilled out walk, bliss...

And, you cannot go to the coast without some good old fish and chips!! They always taste loads better at the coast don't they? Lovely and fresh! You just can't beat it!! Yum, yum, yum!!

It is new settee day!! I am so excited!! We have had a corner suite for years now, and sad as it may be, I cannot wait to get my Christmas Tree up in the corner, near the window, so people can see it from outside!!! Like you do!! Haha!!

The guys deliver it, and unpack it all, put the feet on, and place it wherever you want it! Now, that's good service, usually it is you that has to get rid of all the shite yourself, isn't it?

They put it exactly where I wanted it, and it looks, absolutely gorgeous!! And, the cheeky get says, "bit posh for Cas this, innit love" I said, "what you mean you cheeky get" haha!! We're all a bit posh up here in Cas!!

I saw someone had put something on social media about when you go to Vegas and you think a building is like 2 minutes away, when actually its 10 mile away!!

We did this!!

Jase said, "Kaz, its only there!!" well, we walked, and walked, and walked, and chuffing walked, and still got no closer to where we wanted to be!! Ffs!! What a nightmare!! We were absolutely kanackered!!

School run driving never ceases to amaze me! No one, actually gives a fuck where they park, if they swerve in front of you, and they fly about like absolute nutters with the kids in the car!! It's absolutely unbelievable!! Pure stupidity at the highest level!!!

Well, we are still all worried about this Coronavirus, and most people are doing their utmost to keep safe, and keep those around them safe too, which is an absolute credit to most people.

But, I think what some people are forgetting, is that it's all about reducing the risk!! I feel like I'm back in my old job, doing risk assessments and thinking of ways to reduce the risk, the only difference is, is that if I implemented it in the workplace then it had to be adhered to!!

It is a pity I don't have that control now, because I tell you something it would have been sorted!!

Remember, it is all about reducing the risk...

It's like this 6 people rule, fuck me, it's just all about keeping your circle small isn't it? Is it that hard?? Fucking hell, I haven't even got 6 mates anyway!! Haha!!

'2 police at the door, Good Evening Sir, how many people do you have in there? There are 6 of us, Can we come in and check? Well, no, because that would make it 8'

Fucks sake! #newrules #6 #ruleof6

This has got to be one of the most annoying things ever!! The bin men leaving the bin smack bang in the middle of the drive!! Is it an art?? Do they have training for it? Could you imagine like back in day, when they actually walked down your drive for it, and, carried it on their shoulder!! As if that would ever happen now!!

Lovely Driving Test pass today for one of my pupils.. his sister came driving with me a few years back and passed first time with 0 faults!! Absolutely amazing!! So, obviously no pressure on him then!!!

He only goes and absolutely smashes it!! First time pass, zero faults!! I am absolutely buzzing!! Both siblings, first time passes, zero faults, I am pretty much the dogs doodhas in their house let me tell you!! Oh hi!!

This is so me! And I'm pretty sure any woman can relate to this..

You know a woman is mad at you when she starts a sentence off with, "I just find it funny how..." because there's a 99% chance that she doesn't find it funny at all!! Haha!! Ffs!! So true....

I bought one of them temperature machines today, so I can zap my pupils when they get in the car!! To be fair, it is a pretty serious piece of equipment and, one that I will be using to check their temperatures, and of course my own!! We all need to keep safe!!

And, I have had it on good authority from my nursing friends that if you're menopausal and having a hot do, then your temperature still stays the same, fuck me, not on the inside it doesn't, does it!!

What's with all this 'Karen' shit now too? Like a 'Karen' is a know it all.. I'm actually offended!! Fuck it!! If we now live in a society where we offended by everything, then I am offended by that!! So, there you go!

We pulled up at some traffic lights near a college and the window was down a little bit, for air circulation, and this lad shouts, "ooh look! A real life, Karen!" his mates all looked at me, looked at the name on top of the car, and all started pointing and laughing!!

I thought what a fucking little prick! Haha! Then, one of his mates said, "ooh, the windows down, she's heard you" they all stopped laughing, and I'm just staring at them! We set off, and pass them, and I just nod, and they all burst out lauging!!

My pupil said, "I thought you might have said something!" I said, "well, I was going to, but I found it pretty funny myself, to be fair"

But, then again, us 'Karen's' do know everything, we *do* know best, and, would actually complain about anything!! So, there you go!! #Karen

And once again, we have everyone and their Granny moaning about the Coronavirus Rules!! I've said it before, and I will say it again!!

It is all about reducing the risk! And once people get this into their thick heads, the better it will be!

Surely, it's not just me that gets it, is it?

We are in Tier 2! Thank God! I can still work! I was shitting it in case I had to stop working again! Everyone is back in the zone! Everything is good! It feels like it's all back to a bit of normality!

Well, my Love to Shop Vouchers are here!! I better try and get these spent pretty sharpish before we go into lockdown again!! AND, I might just spend them all on myself this year!!

I go to a Shopping Centre in Leeds with my 400 quid's worth of vouchers and I have every intention of spending them...

Most of the shops still have pretty strict restrictions in place, and I obviously adhere to all the measures, and social distance throughout. I'm thinking of some nice earrings, or a bracelet to buy, so I go to one of the well-known jewellers.

There is a red rope across the door, and there are people inside, so I wait outside at the rope. The shop assistants are chatting away at the counter, they look up, and see me, but just ignore me, which pissed me off to be honest!

Anyway, next thing, one of them asked if they 'can help?' 'can you help?' I want to come in the shop you silly cow!! But, I be polite.. "yes please" I said, she replied, "for what in particular?" I said, "well, I'm not actually sure, maybe earrings or a bracelet, can I just look?"

"you don't know? Well, in that case you will have to wait, the shops full" I thought who the fucks she been clever with? I felt like her off pretty woman! ffs! The snotty cow!! I felt like saying, "hey up love, do you know I've got 400 quid's worth of vouchers here" but instead, I just say, "you know what love, forget it! There's just no need for bad attitude." And off I walk...

I mean, yeah, I get all these restrictions, and I'm a proper stickler for the rules, but some of these shop assistants are on the biggest power trip ever! Pipe the fuck down love!! Haha!!

I have a parcel to pick up from the sorting offie, and their car park, is really small, and tight, so it's always better to reverse in.

I pull into the car park with my roof box on, and start reversing into the parking space, the guy in the car in the next parking space is absolutely shitting it!!

He is stretching right up, leaning over the steering wheel, looking at the front of his car!! Ffs!! I'm the instructor love, not the pupil!! AND, even if it was the pupil then I'm not exactly going to let them bump my car am I never mind yours! Dickhead!!

I have been a Driving Instructor for 11 years!! Woo woo!! I am so pleased that I've done it!

It is a good job, different every day, and people always say, 'do you get bored of driving about all day?' no! is the answer! Because it is a different person every hour, at different stages of their driving, so to be fair, it is pretty interesting and I love it!!

This real funny video popped up on social media today and honestly, it just made me laugh so much!!

It was this guy adding numbers up underneath each other, like we did in the olden days!! Anyway, pretty straightforward, and took about 5 seconds to just add up, and carry up to the next number, add up, done!!

This guy then trots along the whiteboard to do a 'number line' that takes about 10 times longer and utterly confusing!!!

I remember when Sam brought some maths homework home in year 2, and he had to show the working out on a number line. I said, "ooh Sam! I will show you an easier way!" he said, "no mummy! I need to do it this way!" I thought ffs!! What's this shite??

I knew the answer because it was only year 2 maths, but how the fuck do they work it out?? I just didn't have a clue!!

I went into school, and asked his teacher if she could show me how to do a number line? Ffs! How embarrassing!! His teacher said, "oh, it's okay, don't worry, I will show you!" So, there you go! 31 years old, sat in the classroom, whilst a teacher shows me how to do Key Stage 2 number lines!! Haha!!

How true is this???

When you see a mum fretting about how hard the 'toddler stage' is, then don't, under any circumstances, tell her about Year 9!! No way is she ready for this shit!

Ffs! 100% she won't be!!

So, now we have gone up into Tier 3! I can still work, but Jase can't!! ffs!! When is this going to end? And why aren't some people taking this seriously??

Oh no! We are in Lockdown from Monday!!

I have 7 tests booked in, within this lockdown! Ffs! I could cry...

The worse thing is, is that some of these were booked in after the first lockdown and these dates were the only ones available!! I know its shit, but at the same time, we all need to keep safe!!

The tests are rebooked for January and February... fingers crossed we will be able to get enough practice in, and get these tests smashed!!

On the plus side, my hairdresser has rang, and she can fit me in tomorrow before lockdown! Get in! I'm having that!!

When I go to the Salon, its jam packed rammed!! Everyone getting their hair done before this lockdown!!

Well, I will tell you something! My Christmas Tree will be up early this year if I've nothing else to do!!! And, please tell me it's not just me that suffers from P.O.P.D?? Perfect Ornament Placement Disorder??

Omg!! It takes me a lifetime to make sure them baubles are all placed correctly!! I'll sit down, look at it, get up, move it, sit down, look at it, get up, move it, and so on, and so on, and so on!! Ffs! I think it's actually an illness! Haha!!

How funny is I'm a Celeb?? You just know from the start who's going to be doing the challenges!! Haha!!!! It's you!!

Ooh! We are allowed back to work!! We've had a month off, that has absolutely flown by, I better get myself mentally prepared for this!!

I am looking forward to it!! Hopefully not too many will have forgotten what to do!!

We have decided that we will get our milk delivered, in proper bottles, just like the olden days!! I am not sure if this actually right, or I'm just thinking it, but I'm sure this milk tastes loads better out of a bottle and not a carton!! Plus, we are doing our bit for the environment!!

So, Jase has been complaining about his new bank card not been delivered and that it's about to run out. I said, "are you sure you haven't received it?" he said, "no! I would know if I would have received it" okay cocky boots!!

We go to the local shop and his card gets declined! I'm like ffs! How embarrassing!! So, I said to him, "let me look at that card!" it ran out 4 days ago!! Ffs!! Dickhead!! Clearly you can't use it!!

He rings the bank, and she is adamant that they have posted it out!! But anyway, she will post another one out… finally, his new bank card arrives!! All is good!!

A few days later, I am going through our 'recycling' paper, and Jase has this bad habit of not opening his bank statements, which does my head in, but anyway, low and behold, what do I find??? His bank card in an unopened envelope!!

So, basically, he looked at the sender, saw it was from the bank, and chucked it in the recycling!! *You just could not make this shit up!!*

How actually confusing is it when you're on your I-phone and then someone else rings you?? Ffs!! What does it mean?? My brain actually crumbles at this point!! Haha!!

End & Accept

Decline

Hold & Accept

Or ffs!! Aarrghhhh!!

I actually don't know!! How do I even stop it bleeping!! This, has to be one of the most confusing things ever! Not to mention the fact that I have to find my reading glasses to see who it is!! Ffs!! Old Age at its Finest!!

It is my nephews first driving lesson today!! Bless him!! He is so excited!! Not so sure why it took so long for his licence to come like! I think between my sister, and her ex-partner, there was apparently some confusion... erm, more like one blaming the other!! Haha!!

He is so nervous, but we have a good first lesson, and he's just well happy that he didn't stall it!! He can't believe, that he actually drove!! Roll on his next lesson.

Mmm.... How actually nice is a Gingerbread Latte?? Omg!! Sickly as fuck, but, gorgeous and sweet, and full of fat, 6 million calories at the Slimming Club!! Haha!! Good job I am not dieting this month then isn't it??

Chapter Twenty

How actually crazy is all this stuff circulating about the Coronavirus Vaccine?? I mean, come on, the fact that it has got a microchip in so that the government can track what you're doing!! Ffs!! They will be dizzy as fuck tracking me driving round the same routes day in day out!! Haha!!

But, this was the best on social media, pretty much sums it really when the very first lady was vaccinated...

'I wonder how Bill Gates is going to spend his first day in control of Margaret Keenan, 90, from Coventry'

Haha!! Absolute Classic!!

Well Done to Asda closing all its stores on Boxing Day! And rightly so!!

All of them people working their arses off in the pandemic, taking unnecessary shit from stressed out shoppers, and all the time putting themselves at risk of getting the deadly virus too!!

But, to be quite honest, why do they open on Boxing Day anyway? I mean, do people really want to treck around the Asda on Boxing Day? Well, clearly, they do like! But ffs! That is quite sad!!

It really is one of the saddest times visiting the cemetery at Christmas Time, when you can't buy gifts, and all you can do is place flowers on the graves.. it always breaks my heart, and this year is no different.

As I'm leaving, I see someone I know and we start chatting, I look up and this man is looking straight at me, I take a closer look and it's Sam's old headteacher! We exchange 'hellos', and, 'how are you doings', and then he asks about Sam.

I tell him he's all good, and I ask how he is, and then I finish off by saying, "I'm sure will be SO pleased when I tell him I have been chatting to you!" he replies, "I am sure he will Karen!"

We both laugh, knowing full well, that this is *not* the case!

Sam's always been outspoken, and I've always been one of them parents that has had a seat with my name on, in the senior teacher's offices!! Ffs!!

Well, it most certainly will be Christmas with a difference this year! We are having Christmas Dinner on our own, as my nephew is self-isolating, so him and my sister are staying home this year.. it's pretty sad really, but at the same time, it's better to be safe than sorry.

I bet deep down though, there was a lot of families secretly thinking, 'thank fuck all the family can't come' Can you imagine, all the pressure has been taken away from cooking a big, fuck off dinner, and just spending quality time with the immediates!! Not that anyone would openly admit it, the secret is safe with me!!

We go through a housing estate on a lesson today, and there is a spare piece of land and there are 3 young boys playing there.

It's not until we get closer that we see what they have done..

They have only gone and made a 'mud slide' omg! You should have seen the state of them!! They were absolutely covered in mud!! Sliding along on their stomachs!! But, you know what? They were absolutely having the time of their life's!! Go on Lads!! You create some memories, you're only young once!!

Not that I would like to have been their parents washing them clothes!! If it had been Sam, I would have probably thrown them straight in the bin!! Haha!!

Well, this certainly is a Wedding Anniversary with a difference!! Normally we would go away somewhere nice, and have some lovely quality time together... this year we go to Maccy's for a breakfast, and sit in the car park and eat it (change of scenery) haha!!

And then, we buy crap, and sit on the living room floor, whilst we eat it!! It's all making memories, and it will definitely be something to talk about next year!!!

Its Christmas Eve!!

'may you never be too grown up to search the skies on Christmas Eve'

Well, what about the Christmas Eve Jingle at 6pm tonight!! I'm pretty excited to be fair! And, I've bought my own little jingle bell to ring out tonight, along with my neighbours. It will be nice if this becomes a tradition..

Well, Christmas Day is a strange one this year! I suppose it's been the same for a lot of families this year, but, we do all need to keep safe, and hopefully we can all make up for it next year...

It is a 'Grease' and a 'Christmas Carol' kinda day today, 1951 version though!! I absolutely love these 2 films, and I am having a lovely chilled out afternoon, doing exactly what I want to do, which makes a change!! But, sometimes, you just have to do that, don't you?

I get up this morning and there is an empty Gin Bottle in the kitchen! When Jase gets up, I ask him, 'why he has drank all the Gin?' Apparently, it was because we had some ginger ale left!! Ffs!! That's a new one!!

Happy 2021!! Let's see what this Year brings, because, lets face it, no one could have predicted a year like 2020!!

Do men purposely not want to learn how to work the new appliances? Is this so that you will just do it yourself because it is easier? Or, are they just pricks?

Sam didn't know how to put the cooker on, so Jase said, "I will do it for you" about 15 minutes later, Sam said, "Mam, this cooker's not working!" I went in the kitchen, and Jase had only put the grill on instead!! Ffs!! I opened the door and nearly set myself on fire, as well nearly getting blinded, by the smoke!!

The smoke came from the fucking handle that I always rest on the top of the grill when I'm not using it. It had actually melted, onto the grill, and when I tried to take it off the handle snapped in my hand, and the black plastic had well and truly stuck to the grill!! What a dickhead!!

Well, I am surprised to be back at work after the Christmas break, I thought Bozza would have tagged another couple of weeks onto the school holidays, and, put us all back in a mini lockdown.

I am pleased we are back though, it is good to get back to some kind of normality!

Well, that lasted long didn't it! We are all back in lockdown!!

Or well, can't be helped I suppose, we need to keep safe! It seems this second wave and variant is more aggressive and contagious than before, which is, pretty frightening!

I do, actually feel sorry for all the parents that are home schooling, it must be an absolute nightmare!! I for one, would have really struggled with Sam, plus holding down, a full-time job would have been the worst!!

Hats off to you all!!

This did really make me chuckle though...

'And Joe Wicks better not pop back up doing fucking star jumps with the kids at 8 in the morning either, cause he can fuck right off... had enough me!'

My friend does up-cycled furniture, and I've got quite a few pieces in my home, which I absolutely love!! I've seen this absolutely, gorgeous little cabinet that she is selling, that I'm pretty tempted to get, but don't have any room for it!!

I have a small space near my window, I am sure it will fit... oh, surprise, surprise, it does! Well, well, well, that's it! It is bought!! And guess what? It looks amazing!!

Jase's worst nightmare... me sat here with my Homestyle magazine! He just never knows what to expect!! Haha!! I have all these bright ideas that I want in my home, but just haven't even got the space, never mind the money! But, we can dream...

I have never, ever, known anyone fanny about with a log burner like my husband does!! Ffs!! Just make the fucker!! Stop pratting about!! He places all the kindling in a straight line, with no gaps, and then puts loads of firelighters on, and the coal, it actually does surprise me, that it even burns!

I always thought to get a fire going that you needed air? Jase just suffocates and smothers it, never mind lets any air get to it!! It really winds me up big time!!

I thought I would get in the shower tonight and better shave under my arms and legs as I am becoming either a chimp or caveman!! Either way, I am hairy as fuck!!

I just pick any disposable razor up and shave. Omfg!! It is a new bastard razor! I am cut to ribbons!! Ffs!! Blood is running down my legs!! The towel looks like I have been shot, and I look like the biggest dick head with bits of toilet roll stuck on my legs with the blood still seeping through!! That will teach me to use my husband's razor... Hard lesson learnt there, love!!

Yyyaaayyyy!! We have snow!! I am not an absolute lover of it for driving, but for the kids it fab!!

We have a big field at the back of us and it was lovely to see families enjoying themselves, making snowmen, little snowball fights and generally having some good quality family time.

Just keep making those memories...

And, one of our neighbours is the best! We have a grit bin at the top of our hill, and he always grits the hill and our street, bless him! He's a 'goodun' is Neil!!

Why does every channel need to show the American Presidents Inauguration?? That is my routine well and truly out of the window today!!

The routine is:

Lingo, which I am actually quite good at!!

Tipping point, which Jase hates, and I'm like "whoa, look at all them, ready to drop" and Jase just does not share my enthusiasm!!

The Chase, which again, I love, I bet The Chasers are dying to really laugh !! It is so funny!!

I reckon I could go on any one of these shows and piss it! But then again, maybe I couldn't!! haha!!

This has got be one of the funniest quotes, and also at this moment in time, one of the most true ones!

We are all in need of a holiday...

'Remember when you all used to look down your noses at holidays in Benidorm, now you would all give your right tit to be down that strip in the sunshine drinking shit cocktails wondering what's going to come out of Sticky Vicky's fanny next!'

Ffs! Wouldn't we just... never mind, one day, hopefully soon, we will not take our freedom for granted again..

Well, I've heard it all today!! Apparently, there is a petition going around, for Driving Instructors to be able to conduct Driving Tests, instead of the Examiners!! Well, clearly this will never happen in a month of Sundays!!

This is my latest status...

'My ability to now scroll by absolute bell end, dick head statuses, and just laugh, instead of commenting, has become my greatest lockdown 3 achievement!!'

I mean, let's face it, this past year has really shown people's true colours!

Now, don't get me wrong, we are all entitled to our own opinions, and we are never always going to agree, and, that's what makes us all who we are, what makes us unique, and, I'm all for that, but some people just need to get a life!!

So, today marks 1 year from the first Coronavirus case, who would have thought that it would have ripped through our country like it did, who would have thought over 100,000 people would have lost their lives to it, who would have thought that all these families would be grieving like they are, who would have thought, that, in this day and age, people would be dying alone in hospital, with no family around them, who would have thought that this was even possible...

Who would have thought that the government would pay us to stay at home, who would have thought they would furlough staff, who would have thought the self-employed would get paid to stay home, who would have thought businesses would close and be paid, who would have thought that this was even possible...

Well, a year ago, we wouldn't have would we, but, 2020 has been like no other year ever, and, we have certainly lived through a time that will go down in history.

Let us not take anything in life for granted anymore, and, in a world where you can be anything, be kind.

You just couldn't make it up...

Keep Safe and Much Love xxx

Printed in Great Britain
by Amazon